Sex Ed
~~Human Interaction~~
with Mrs. Gladys B. Furley, R.N.

EXPECTING
the
UNEXPECTED

Sex Ed

~~Human Interaction~~

with Mrs. Gladys B. Furley, R.N.

EXPECTING THE

Unexpected

By Mavis Jukes

Delacorte Press
New York

Published by
Delacorte Press
Bantam Doubleday Dell Publishing Group, Inc.
1540 Broadway
New York, New York 10036

Library of Congress Cataloging-in-Publication Data
Jukes, Mavis.
Human Interaction with Mrs. Gladys B. Furley, R.N. : expecting the
unexpected / Mavis Jukes.
p.   cm.
Summary: Twelve-year-old River and her sixth-grade classmates handle the
information from their sex education class in different ways, and it leads River
to the conclusion that her older sister's unusual behavior is due to pregnancy.
ISBN 0-385-32242-9 (alk. paper)
[1. Schools—Fiction.   2. Family life—Fiction.   3. Sisters—Fiction.]   I. Title.
PZ7.J9294Hu   1996
[Fic]—dc20   96-2464
CIP
AC

The text of this book is set in 12.75-point Baskerville No. 2.

Book design by Lilian Rosenstreich

Manufactured in the United States of America

October 1996

10   9   8   7   6   5   4   3   2   1

For Jaimi, Bill and Grady

One

RIVER WANDERED through the living room. Her older sister, Megan, was asleep on the couch with her geometry book on her chest and the radio on. Megan's geometry book seemed like a little tent, one that had magical sleep-inducing properties. And she'd been snoozing under it on a regular basis for the past few weeks.

Megan had been so tired lately! Tired and grumpy, and with a bellyache undoubtedly associated with her you-know-what.

River looked at Megan's beautiful frowning eyebrows and eyelids dusted with brown eye shadow. She looked at Megan's beautiful frowning mouth. Gosh. She was grouchy even in her sleep.

River moved closer. What color lipstick was Megan wearing?

Megan snorted, and River jumped back. She tiptoed to the light switch and turned the lights down a little. Let Her Premenstrual Majesty sleep, thought River. She slowly faded the music out.

Maybe sometime later on in the month, River would ask to borrow Megan's lipstick.

River went into her bedroom. Her Madame Eloise makeup kit was open on her dresser. She lifted her bangs and looked at herself in the mirror for a minute before closing the lid.

Then she went into the bathroom and found the small plastic bottle of makeup remover. She removed the tiny bit of mascara she'd borrowed from Megan without asking. She washed her face and smeared some OXY5 on a group of small red bumps on her forehead.

She stared at herself in the mirror. Was she pretty or not? She didn't know. She had pretty green eyes with brown flecks in them. She had pretty permed hair. She had a small brown mole high up on one cheek that was supposed to be a beauty mark. Maybe she was pretty.

But she wasn't pretty like Kirstin Walker.

And she wasn't going to be one of the six people going to Kirstin's party on Saturday. But so what? Why should River care about a party in a limo with Cokes and a TV in it?

River squeezed a blob of toothpaste onto Megan's toothbrush—she didn't see her own.

The kids at Kirstin's party were going to get all dressed up and cruise around town. They would make a run to the border for Taco Bell, go to Bud's for ice cream, go to Pacific Cinemas, and then everybody would be taken home.

"I'm sorry!" Kirstin had told River apologetically after she had passed out the invitations. "I could only invite six people. My mom said! You were my seventh choice," she added. Then Kirstin offered to stop by River's house in the limo in case River wanted to see everybody all dressed up.

River spat in the sink and rinsed her mouth by sucking fresh water from the toothbrush a few times. She dried the bristles with a hand towel and put it back exactly where the Royal Queen of PMS had left it—upside down on the counter near the sink.

She leaned down and looked under the marble washstand at a gigantic purple box of Kotex pads that her mom had gotten at Price Club. Too bad! It still hadn't been opened.

River's Human Interaction teacher, Mrs. Furley, had suggested that the girls who hadn't started their periods might wear a pad around for a couple of hours to try it out. "Just put one in your underwear and take it for a spin," she had said. "But do *not* try a tampon," Mrs. Furley had

3

warned them. "Tampons used incorrectly can make you ill."

This was no surprise to River, since just the idea of using a tampon made her ill. Imagine poking a cotton plug with a string attached up inside your body! What if it got lost?

River did, however, want to take a pad for a spin.

In fact, she'd been waiting for weeks to take a pad for a spin.

But there was no way she was going to open up a whole new gigantic purple box of ninety-six individually wrapped Kotex maxipads to do that. Since River's mother had gone through menopause, Megan would wonder who had opened the box and why one was missing.

So River would wait until Megan had opened the box and used a few pads. Then she'd take one for herself and waddle around in it for a while.

River went back into her room. She carefully moved everything off her bed, except her cat, Helene. She refolded her student council rep sweatshirt. She ate the last crumbs from a bag of Salsa Rio chips and put the bag in the trash.

She straightened the line of nail polishes on her dresser top so that they were arranged from pinks to dark pinks to reds to red browns. She put her shoes side by side, toes sticking under the bed.

River checked to make sure the blinds were absolutely, positively closed. She took off her shirt and pants and opened her closet door and stuffed them into the large black mailbox she used for a hamper. She checked the blinds again. Then she took off her bra and hid it in her underwear drawer.

She put on the sheer white nightgown her grandma had sent her and stopped to stare at herself in the mirror. Gosh! How old did her grandma think she was, five? What good was a nightie that showed things right through the fabric? Who designed such a stupid gown?

Luckily, she'd snagged her dad's new XXL T-shirt out of the clean laundry basket before Megan could find it. She put it on over her nightgown and stretched it all the way down to her knees. Tomorrow she'd put the Grandma nightgown through the wash and give it to her mother to give to the Salvation Army. Maybe a small, short wife would want to buy it and wear it for her husband.

To spark a little human interaction.

River crept into bed and snuggled deep into the covers, careful not to move her toes and get Helene into hunting mode.

River wished somebody in her family had bought six raffle tickets for a dollar at the school fundraiser and won a limo ride for six for three hours the way Kirstin's mother had. Why had Kirstin's family won? They had a boat and a trailer to pull it on, a Land Cruiser and a new Lexus convertible with gold wheels. And a pool with a cabana. And aqua wall-to-wall carpeting!

River rubbed her nose. It had been three years

since she'd worn the retainer with a prong on the top to make her quit sucking her thumb, but every once in a while it crossed her mind to take a little nip off it. She shoved her hand under her pillow for safekeeping.

Soon Megan's boyfriend, Anton, would have his driver's license and the occasional use of his parents' tan Ford. River would rather be seen cruising around town with her two *real* friends, Candace and Jules, and a totally buff guy who wore his hat backward, and her continuously premenstrually stressed big sister—even in a tan Ford—than with a bunch of jerky trendoid celebrity wannabes sucking on jawbreakers in a limousine.

She turned her head on the pillow. Mrs. Furley would be coming to her classroom at ten-forty-five the next morning. River smiled, a little, to herself.

According to the course outline, the section about boys' personal stuff would soon begin.

Ha! thought River.

Let them suffer.

Let them suffer, the way the girls had through the girl stuff, through the continuous flow of period information, which had gone on for *five consecutive classes*—at least.

Periods this and periods that. Irregular periods when you first started, and irregular periods when you finally stopped.

Missed periods when you were pregnant.

Missed, because the bloody fluid was somehow

to nourish a developing embryo. Sick! How could an embryo get that hungry?

The one good thing River was able to report about periods was that they eventually stopped. Good old menopause! Too bad you had to wait until you were fifty to dry up!

River's mother had been luckier than most, and River hoped this good luck would run in the family: Her mother had started her period when she was fourteen and a half and ended it recently at age forty-three. This she had reported to the family at dinner, of all places: that she'd had some spotting and then no period at all.

Spotting! What would ever possess the woman to discuss this in front of a plate of pasta primavera, her husband, and her two kids?

River sighed deeply, thinking back on it. There was no one on God's green earth less embarrassable than her mother.

Except Mrs. Gladys B. Furley, R.N.

Last year, after a brief skirmish at the school board meeting and a vote at Franklin School, and several heated debates about the curriculum, the Human Interaction Program had been born. Gladys Furley, formerly the district nurse, had been chosen to teach the course.

Mrs. Furley had no known limits regarding what she was willing to explain, with or without being asked. For example: the "Pad Fest" she had sponsored—featuring overnights, maxis, slims, thins and minis, and, incredible as it seemed, winged pads.

Wings? For what purpose?

River had no idea. But winged pads had been prominently displayed on the counter for anybody who wanted a closer look.

Which was, of course, nobody.

Except Margaret Rothrock.

A car pulled into the driveway, and a moment later River heard a key turn in the lock. She heard her parents walk in. "Girls?" said River's mother. She appeared in the doorway of River's bedroom.

"I know you had lemon torte for dessert," said River. "And didn't bring me any."

"I did not."

"Let me smell your breath," said River.

Her mother crossed the rug. "I only split one small piece of raspberry cheesecake with Dad and had an espresso, I swear it," she said. "Sweet dreams," she whispered. She kissed River good-night.

River could see the shadow of her father in the doorway.

"Did you put Helene out?" asked her mother.

River pretended not to hear her.

River's father took off one loafer and flipped it and caught it. He took off the other one and stuffed them both under his arm. He walked in and sat on the edge of River's bed and brushed her bangs away from her forehead. He looked into her eyes. "I'll be gone when you wake up in the morning," he said. "But I'll be back before you know it."

River's mother loudly sighed.

"Just a short plane hop from Oakland to Reno, one day touring the mine, a quick Jeep ride back to the Reno airport, and I'll be home on Wednesday. By noon." He glanced at River's mother. "I promise."

"Well, please bring me back lemon meringue pie from the airport coffee shop," River said. "And Dad?"

"What."

"It's gross to sit around with loafers wedged in your armpit."

River's parents went into the living room. A moment later River heard Her Majesty say sleepily, "Leave me alone! I'm working on my geometry!"

After a while, River grew tired of Helene's loudly purring and kneading River's stomach with her awful little prickly claws. Helene would have to go out. River got up and picked up the cat, very gently, because of the many icky lumpy bumps in Helene's belly, which would one day be kittens. River held Helene against her chest and chin and snuck down the hall, past the living room door. She saw her parents still standing there, watching Megan sleep.

"What's going on?" whispered River.

"Oh, we were just remembering Megan's first car," whispered River's mother. "It was a big plastic high-topped tennis shoe with red wheels and a little seat that opened up, with a storage compartment . . ."

"Now she wants a black Honda!" whispered River's dad.

"She used to keep animal crackers in the compartment," whispered River's mother. "Soon she'll have her license and will be toodling off down the road all by herself. And next, she'll be going off to college—"

"Good," said River.

"At ten thousand dollars a pop, per semester!" whispered River's dad. "And everybody complains that I work too much!"

River's mother looked at him. "I only said that it's very, *very* important that you be home for our meeting on Wednesday afternoon!"

Megan opened her eyes halfway. "And I want the Honda to have tinted windows," she told her dad. She closed her eyes again.

River quietly opened the back door and set Helene on the ground. The rain had stopped. The street was dark and quiet; the moon was halfway sunk into the clouds. River's mother came over and stood behind her.

"Is everything okay with you and Dad?" said River.

"Why do you ask?" said her mother.

"Because this morning I heard you tell Dad that you were sick of his being a geologist and being gone all the time."

"This morning I was," said her mother.

"And then tonight you were arguing again!" said River.

"We weren't arguing. We were discussing. I'm making sure he doesn't get waylaid by those loony Canadian prospectors again. They don't seem to understand that your father has family obligations! He can't roar around in the slush in some fancy company Jeep! Last trip, they buried it up to the axles!"

"Well, it scares me when you're mad at Dad," said River.

River's mother put her arms around River's shoulders and rested her chin on the top of River's head and they stood there in the doorway, breathing the fresh, damp, dark night air.

"I love Dad," said River quietly.

"Me too," said River's mom. "And I don't want you to worry about anything. Dad and I promised: '. . . till death do us part . . . for richer, for poorer, in sickness and in health . . .' "

River leaned back against her mother.

". . . through thin thighs and through fat thighs . . ."

"Mom, shhh," said River.

They looked out into the night.

"Mom?"

"What."

"Is it okay if I have that little mini–sewing kit you ripped off the Hilton?"

"I did *not* rip off anything from the Hilton! Those kits are complimentary."

"Well, can I have it?"

"Yes."

"Good."

"For what?"

"Nothing."

Two

RIVER'S SIXTH-GRADE CLASS was tied for first place for the Franklin School First Annual Class With Class Award. And River really wanted to win!

The class that won the award would get: (1) a pizza party; (2) a trip to Scandia to play miniature golf and use the batting machines; (3) a special group class photo, which would be framed and displayed outside the office for one year; (4) its teacher's name inscribed on a brass plaque mounted inside the office; and (5) no homework for an entire week.

Every upper-grade class had started the contest with 200 points. Bonus points were added to this total score for outstanding efforts toward improving the appearance of the school in general; points were deducted from the total score for each and every infraction.

An example of an infraction would be doing homework for another subject during Human Interaction.

But River was a good sneak and an excellent student, and Mrs. Furley would never suspect her. Plus, her classroom teacher, Mr. Elmo, had left—as he always did—when Mrs. Furley came to the room.

So, during Human Interaction, River occasionally looked up at Mrs. Furley with a pleasant, innocent expression as she did the fractions review sheet she'd snuck into her binder.

"River?" said Mrs. Furley.

River jumped.

"Can you review for the class what the word *ovulation* means?"

There was a loud sigh from the back of the room.

It was Margaret.

River turned back a few pages in her binder and glanced at her notes. Why me? she thought.

"It's when 'a tiny egg is released from an egg sac that has moved to the outer edges of an ovary,' " she read.

"Right," said Mrs. Furley. "Margaret? What's the problem?"

"The problem is," said Margaret, "that we've been over and over all of this material. I'm sick of egg sacs and estrogen—and last week you said we'd be moving on."

"All in good time, Margaret," said Mrs. Furley. "We haven't fully covered the topic of pregnancy, and today we're having our short review section, as is clearly stated in the course outline. Have you checked your course outline recently?"

"No," said Margaret. "All I know is what you promised us last week."

"So then what happens to the egg?" said Mrs. Furley to River.

River looked again at her notes. "It's moved by little hairs down a fallopian tube toward the uterus?"

"Bravo!" said Mrs. Furley. "Then what happens?"

River shrugged.

"Who would you like to help you with the answer?" said Mrs. Furley.

River glanced around the room. She looked at Candace, who frowned and shook her head no.

"I would like Candace to help me," said River.

"Pass," said Candace.

River looked at Jules.

"No!" mouthed Jules.

"I would like Jules to help me," said River.

"I don't know either!" cried Jules. She looked around the room. "But I would recommend that DB help."

River looked over at DB. Gosh. He looked great

in his Nike T-shirt! And what a great profile he had, looking down at his notebook.

"Well," said DB, "*if* it's fertilized, it cruises into the uterus and parks itself in the lining of the uterus and chills for nine months."

"What is this 'fertilizer' stuff?" mumbled Margaret, leafing through her notes.

"And what if it *doesn't* get fertilized?" Mrs. Furley asked DB. "It disintegrates. Remember? And a couple of weeks later, the uterus sheds its lining . . . a process which is called what?"

Nobody answered.

"Henry? You know this!"

"I do?" said Henry.

"Yes. When the uterus sheds its lining, what's it called?" asked Mrs. Furley.

"PMS!" said Henry. "Otherwise known as flipping out for a week and having temper tantrums or crying during cookie commercials like my mom does."

"Henry?" said Mrs. Furley. "Think . . . about . . . the . . . question. We're not talking about premenstrual syndrome here. It's a simple question: *What* is it called when the uterus sheds its lining?"

"Being on the rag," said Henry.

"More politely referred to as . . ."

Henry stared at her.

". . . more politely referred to as menstruation, Henry," said Mrs. Furley. "Please use appropriate

16

terminology. We've been over this many, many times."

"*What* is the fertilizer?" cried Margaret.

Several students turned around to look at her.

"Calm down, Margaret," said Mrs. Furley. "And stay with the group. Okay, Margaret?" She smiled at Margaret a little. "But here's a review question for *you:* If a fertilized egg should happen to implant itself in the lining of the uterus, would the woman have her next period?"

Margaret stared at her. "I'm not answering because you won't tell me what the fertilizer is."

"Would she or wouldn't she?" said Mrs. Furley in a firm voice.

Margaret kept quiet.

Mrs. Furley took a deep breath. "The woman wouldn't have a period, Margaret, because the lining of the uterus is needed to nourish an embryo as it grows," she said. She pointed to what was written on the board. "And *that*," she said, "is why missing a period is one of the first outward signs of pregnancy." She picked up a chalkboard eraser. "Is everyone done copying this?"

"No!" cried almost everybody.

"Then take a few more minutes. Those of you who are done may review notes and can come up and ask any questions you may have—or put a written question in the question basket."

River continued copying notes from the board in her beautiful, neat handwriting.

Mrs. Furley pointed at Margaret and motioned for her to come up to her desk. Margaret tiptoed up. "Look, Margaret," whispered Mrs. Furley kindly. "I know you're eager for answers, but there's a method to my madness. I've developed my course outline so that all of the information will come together in a logical way."

"But I'm just confused about what the fertilizer is," whispered Margaret.

River glanced at Candace, who closed her eyes and slowly shook her head.

"Male reproductive cells, Margaret," said Mrs. Furley quietly. "Remember? That reside within the male's reproductive organs. I said we'd get into that in detail very soon."

"But I've been wondering and wondering—how would cells from a guy get all the way up those little hairy tubes?"

Someone in the back of the room groaned.

"Soon, Margaret," said Mrs. Furley. "I promise . . . male reproductive stuff. Coming right up!"

"But—"

"I'll tell you *every last* detail, my word of honor," said Mrs. Furley. "Please, Margaret, let's take this one step at a time. Have a seat."

Margaret stopped for a moment at the question basket. She helped herself to one of the small slips of paper that were stacked beside it, picked up the pencil that was tied to a string and thumbtacked to the counter beside it, and scribbled: WHAT IS THE FERTILIZER!

She folded the paper in half and dropped it into the basket.

Then she marched to her seat.

River copied notes about placentas and embryos.

Finally she got to the last paragraph; good thing, because her fingernail was digging into her palm. "After nine months," she copied, "if all goes well, the pregnant woman will begin the process of childbirth, called labor. The baby will pass from her body into the world."

River stopped to think about this for a moment.

Oh well, I can always adopt, she thought, and closed her notebook.

Her stomach grumbled.

How long before this dumb class was over so she could eat? Suddenly Mrs. Furley stood up. "Oops! I forgot today's Brain Tickler!" She picked up the chalk and wrote: LIST TEN CHANGES ASSOCIATED WITH PREGNANCY.

"Number one," whispered Henry. "Growing bigger honkers!"

Peter snorted.

Mrs. Furley looked over her shoulder at Henry. "Excuse me?" she said.

Henry said nothing.

"Isn't this class neck and neck with Mrs. Hansen's class for first place in the Class With Class contest?"

"Yes," said Henry.

"Well, are you aware that I am one of the teachers evaluating your class?"

"Yes," said Henry. "I am!"

"Well, *so far,* this class hasn't lost a single point from me. Everyone's doing a marvelous job of listening to each other and encouraging each other, and not putting down each other's questions and answers, *but* we can do without the honker talk, Henry. I expect you to use proper terms as much as possible, and I don't know how I can make this any more clear to you."

"All I said was that I saw two Canadian honkers flying south for the winter!" said Henry.

"Oh yes, Henry, I'm *sure* that's what you said," Mrs. Furley answered. She slid her glasses down to the end of her nose with one finger and peered at him for a long moment.

Then she sat down at Mr. Elmo's desk and began looking through papers in her briefcase. Behind Mrs. Furley was a long bank of windows that opened up onto the covered breezeway. The breezeway went along the outside of the classrooms. It connected the clusters of classrooms, the office, and the multipurpose room. River stared out the windows.

What a horrible design!

River decided that if she grew up to be an architect, she would vote to lift the license of any architect who designed such a tacky, ugly breezeway.

In the central courtyard, a few soggy leaves still hung on to the branches of some ornamental trees; muddy footprints had squashed the grass around the terrace. Certainly River could think of a way to improve the school's appearance! And get bonus points for her class.

She set to work making a sketch for a design around the windows of her classroom that would look good on the outside wall.

She heard Henry whisper, "Okay, then. Number one: Growing bigger *hooters!*"

"That is *not* a sign of pregnancy," whispered Margaret.

"Yes it is!" said Henry.

"No it isn't!" said Margaret.

"It is too," whispered Henry. "My aunt's pregnant, and she can balance a whole tea set on 'em."

"She can not!" cried Margaret.

Mrs. Furley frowned at the class.

Everyone got quiet again.

Mrs. Furley closed her briefcase. Then she got up and strolled around the room. "Wonderful display!" she said quietly, looking at the "I Have a Dream" bulletin board.

"River designed it," volunteered Margaret. "And we all hope you'll take careful note of it for the Class With Class Award."

"Good for you, River," said Mrs. Furley.

"And she's the one who drew the picture of Dr. King," said Margaret.

"Well, keep up the good work—all of you," said Mrs. Furley. "A class with class has pride in all aspects of the classroom, including the art displays. Ah!" she said. "There's Mrs. McPhearson. Excuse me a minute."

Mrs. Furley went to the doorway and flagged down Mrs. McPhearson, the principal. They chatted for a moment outside the door. Then Mrs. McPhearson clicked her clip-on sunglasses into the up position and looked into the room. "You're doing a wonderful job!" she told the class. "Oops! I'm on in five minutes!"

She shook hands with Mrs. Furley and booked it down the breezeway.

"Mrs. McPhearson and I were just talking about the AIDS Awareness Fund-raiser last week," said Mrs. Furley. "Her son-in-law was there, heading things up. He's a gynecologist—remember what a gynecologist is?"

River couldn't believe it! The principal's son-in-law was a gynecologist? How would you like to have a gynecologist in the family?

River sighed and shook her head. Suddenly her dad's poking around in holes in the desert didn't seem so bad after all.

"Anyway," Mrs. Furley continued, "we'll discuss HIV and other sexually transmitted diseases toward the end of the course."

"And in the meantime, don't sit on any toilet seats," Margaret said. "Right?"

"Wrong," said Mrs. Furley.

"Well, my cousin Helen got teeny little itchy crayfish hatching all over herself from sitting on her friend's toilet seat," mumbled Margaret.

"Crabs, Margaret," said Mrs. Furley, "not crayfish. And that's a *very* unusual way to catch crabs.

22

And *might* I add that I doubt that your cousin Helen would appreciate your sharing this little tidbit with the class?"

"Why not?" said Margaret. "She didn't know her friend had bugs in her fur that jumped onto the toilet seat! It wasn't *Helen's* fault!"

"I didn't say it was!" said Mrs. Furley. "I'm just saying: Don't put it on the ten o'clock news!"

Three

THE LUNCH BELL rang.

Mr. Elmo limped back into the classroom.

"Hello, Frank!" said Mrs. Furley. "Your class was marvelous—for the most part." She eyeballed Henry for a moment before gathering her things.

"Well, I have nothing but the highest expectations of these people," said Mr. Elmo. "Of course, I'd love to know who sabotaged my stadium boots by putting newspaper in the toes," he added.

He glanced at DB.

River felt a little pang of guilt deep in her chest. Had the stadium boots really pinched his toes badly enough to make him limp like that?

No.

The Elmo Dog was faking it.

He was faking it, and that was all there was to it.

She dug in her pack for the little Hilton sewing kit and concealed it in her hand. On the way out of the room, she pretended to bump into Noah and took the opportunity to slyly tuck the packet of needles and thread, and teensy scissors, into the pocket of Noah's cardigan sweater. "Go for it," she told him.

"Your wish is my command!" he whispered to her out of the side of his mouth.

River headed down the hall with Candace. Candace put her hand on River's arm to stop her. "Listen. Is that Los Lobos playing?"

Margaret hurried past, wearing her green Little Mermaid backpack. "What's the haps?" Margaret called out. She didn't wait for an answer.

Poor Margaret, with her Disney watch and barrettes; River figured she'd hit puberty sometime past the turn of the century.

River and Candace walked faster. Jules caught up with them. What on earth was going on? They followed some other students into the multipurpose room. There, while fifty or sixty lower-graders lined up for sloppy joes, green Jell-O and milk, Mrs. McPhearson was belting out her rendition of "La Bamba" on a video karaoke machine. There was a TV on a cart beside her. The words "PARA BAILAR

LA BAMBA NECESITA UNA POCA DE GRACIA"
moved across the screen below some flashy-looking
dancers.

A third-grader who rode River's bus stood close
to the door with her hands over her ears. River
leaned down and asked her, "What are we talking
about here?"

The girl frowned at her. *"What?"*

"What's going on?" said Jules. "What's happen-
ing here?"

"Mrs. McPhearson didn't believe the lower-
graders could read ten thousand pages in the Read-
A-Thon," the girl shouted. "So she said if they
reached the ten thousand goal, she'd either eat her
hat or rent a singing machine from Home Video
and sing 'La Bamba.' " The girl made a sour face.
"She claims she doesn't have a hat, so now we have
to put up with this."

Most of the kids in the line stood politely, looking down at their shoes and saying nothing. The
few who had already gotten their lunches just
stared and chewed. One boy was laughing uproari-
ously, with milk squirting out of his nose.

River smiled to herself. Good Old Mrs.
McPhearson! What a class act. Look at her, would
you? Closing her eyes and singing! And rocking out!
And what was this? A little action in the hips? Good
old, funny old Mrs. McPhearson—you had to love
her.

But you wouldn't want to mess with her.

"If the sixth-graders promise to read ten thousand pages," Candace whispered as they headed out together, "do you think we can get her to shut up?"

The sun was out in a small space of blue. River squinted at the yard to check out the scenery. No DB yet. Too bad; the Deebster would have improved the landscape considerably.

The girls found an empty picnic table and sat down and began prowling through their lunches. River and Candace watched as Jules began pulling out and lining up a parade of delicious-looking items: chicken wings cooked in soy sauce, two puffy buns with barbecued pork inside. Sliced apples, orange sections, two almond cookies . . .

Brother!

Now she was hauling out a small container of macaroni salad with pink shrimp in it. Next: a preserved plum in a double paper wrapper. Then out came a napkin with Minnie Mouse printed on it, a plastic spoon and fork and two small paper packets: salt and pepper. And a carton of cranberry juice!

Boy!

River wished her mom and dad could come up with something more inventive for lunch than cheese sandwiches.

Kirstin Walker came out into the yard with a small herd of Kirstin groupies, undoubtedly some of the limo invitees. She waved to River, and River waved back. "It's my mood ring," Kirstin was saying to Stella as they passed by. She held it out for Stella to admire. "See? It's pink," said Kirstin. "It means I'm feeling passionate."

She looked over at one of the boys and laughed.

Kirstin and her entourage found a good spot in the grass; Kirstin got comfortable in the center of the group. She sat with her eyes closed and her face toward the sun, trying to bag a few rays.

Since Kirstin's eyes were closed, River spied on her.

Boy, was Kirstin pretty! And she seemed to be getting prettier every year.

River watched as Kirstin undid her ponytail and shook her hair so that it tumbled down her back— just as DB walked by. Kirstin must have been peeking!

That sneak!

River stabbed a little pink shrimp in the macaroni salad with Jules's fork and ate it.

"All Kirstin knows about or cares about is limo parties and Lexus cars," said Jules. She took back her fork.

"That's not true," said River.

River took a drink of Jules's juice. "Didn't you read her Martin Luther King language arts paper?"

"No," said Jules.

River smiled a little. "Well, read it. I put it up right in the middle of the dream display. Kirstin has a dream. And the dream is about a black BMW. So!" said River, helping herself to a large bite of Jules's puffy bun. "She doesn't just care about limos and Lexuses. She also cares about other kinds of cars."

"There's pork in that puffy bun!" said Jules.

"Not anymore," said River. She took another long drink of juice, and Jules grabbed the carton back.

Mr. Elmo came out into the yard holding a mug with a picture of a fighter plane on it. He sat on an empty picnic table and put his feet on the bench.

River pretended to hide behind her lunch bag. Then she peeked out and waved. Mr. Elmo waved back.

What a sweet guy!

And, because he was such a sweet guy, everybody loved Mr. Elmo.

And, because they loved him, they only tortured him a very little bit.

Each and every day.

They had to! Because they were sixth-graders.

Torturing Elmo was their job.

"Your toes seem to have recovered!" River called to Mr. Elmo.

"No they haven't," said Mr. Elmo.

"You didn't limp out here," called River.

"Yes I did," said Mr. Elmo. He got up and limped off in the direction of the teachers' lunchroom.

"Who did you give the needle and thread assignment to?" Candace whispered to River.

"Noah," whispered River.

"Why Noah?"

"He won second place at the fair last summer," said River, "for an embroidered trout on a spoonbill cap. Believe me. The boy will get the job done."

Four

RIVER HAD A FLEA BITE that was itching high on the upper back part of her leg. She broke away from Jules and Candace and caught up to some fourth-graders carrying a boom box and danced along with them a little; this provided some temporary relief from the itching. But dancing gave her a wedgie, and there was no place to hide and fix it.

And no time to run to the girls' room before the bell rang.

River was sick of wedgies!

If she grew up to become a famous clothing de-signer and owned a big company, she would fire ev-ery last employee who couldn't design underwear leg holes that stayed where they belonged.

But for now, she would call her mom and ask her to pick her up after school and take her shopping for different underwear. River needed new undies. And a nightgown that wasn't see-through.

She jammed her hand into her pocket and scratched her thigh.

And she needed *not* to sleep with Helene anymore.

That pregnant fleabag!

She walked into the classroom.

"River?" said Mr. Elmo.

Now what?

"Pop quiz!" Mr. Elmo cried. "Langston Hughes! James Baldwin! Lorraine Hansberry! Gwendolyn Brooks! Paul Laurence Dunbar! Alice Walker! What do they have in common? They're all writers!"

I knew that, thought River.

Margaret raised her hand. "You didn't give River a chance to answer!"

"During lunch, I was browsing through my grade book," said Mr. Elmo. "One person and one person only has turned in every history assignment this month, and that person is Noah. Noah? Where are you?"

Mr. Elmo glanced around the room.

"I'm in here!" Noah said, poking his head out of the doorway of the computer room. "And Mr. Elmo? Please leave me alone! You said I could work on the computer!"

Mr. Elmo sighed. "And let me also discuss something else: How many of you have brought in novels, biographies, autobiographies for Sustained Silent Reading? And how many are choosing to do the minimum, instead, reading comic books and magazine articles?"

"You sleep during Sustained Silent Reading!" cried Margaret.

"Well, what do you expect?" said Mr. Elmo. "You wear me out with all the nonsense!"

"Well, I'm reading a book," said Margaret.

"What book?"

"Never mind," said Margaret.

"Pop quiz!" cried Mr. Elmo. "*The Color Purple:* movie? Or book? Both! Why are we learning about Alice Walker? Because it's Black History Month? Wrong! Because she's a distinguished American writer!"

"You still won't give anybody time to answer!" cried Margaret.

"Well, get that hand up faster!"

"I had my hand up but you didn't call on me!"

Mr. Elmo ignored Margaret. "All of you—get with it. You want the Class With Class Award? If you don't start getting these history assignments in, it's going to be points off, points off, points off.

"In junior high," he added, "you don't get a second chance to get assignments in without getting your grade knocked down a peg or two."

He took off his Orioles cap and ran his hand backward across the top of his head, then put the cap on again.

"Or getting a big, fat zero. What do you think

they do in junior high, hold your hand everywhere you go? You think a little angel sits on your shoulder and says 'Do this! Do that! Don't forget to blow your nose!'?"

He took off his cap again. "Has this cap shrunk or has my head grown bigger?" He put it on again and turned it backward. "Ouch! I'm pulling my own hair out!"

What hair? thought River.

"Ouch! Darn it! Who readjusted this plastic band? You don't think I know it goes in the number one hole?"

He stared at DB.

"I thought you said no hats in class," said Margaret.

"I said no hats in class unless you're the teacher. As it happens, Madam Cop, my head is cold. Not all of us are twelve years old and in the sixth grade. Consequently, Margaret, not all of us have the benefit of a complete head of hair."

Mr. Elmo turned and started to write something on the board but changed his mind.

"And by the way. To the person who stuffed paper in the toes of my stadium boots . . . ," he said, glaring at DB, "I would like to say that pinching my feet into those boots for a half-mile hike home before I discovered your little prank may ultimately cost me a sixty-five-dollar trip to the podiatrist. These little gags can backfire, people! When I walked to my house in them yesterday, I irritated my big toenail, which was squeezed in a bad way."

Mr. Elmo turned to the board.

"PODIATRIST," he wrote. "Look it up!"

Mr. Elmo seemed to be getting madder by the minute. "Knock off the childish pranks! Knock off the pranks at the expense of others!"

River glanced into the computer room and saw Mr. Elmo's blue blazer moving. Noah was in there, busy as a beaver.

She could see the hanger rocking back and forth. Soon the job would be complete.

And what an excellent job the Noah Boy would do.

Noah would do an excellent job, and the class would have advanced its plan one more peg. The plan was to alter Mr. Elmo's clothing seven different ways in seven days. It was day five, and things had been going well.

But this afternoon River had developed mixed feelings about the goal.

Mr. Elmo was acting pretty marginal.

Maybe the needle and thread plan wasn't such a good idea after all. Maybe they'd played enough tricks on Mr. Elmo.

River gazed through the window into the computer room.

And at that moment Noah slowly raised his head and looked at her, his eyes twinkling.

Then he ducked down again.

Don't be ridiculous, River told herself. There's no such thing as too many tricks on Mr. Elmo. The needle and thread plan was an excellent idea—excellent!

Candace raised her hand. "We love you, Mr. Elmo!" she told him. "And we're very sorry your piggies got squished."

The class grew quiet.

"Well, I enjoy an occasional prank," said Mr. Elmo. "But today I'm upset. I see the lack of interest in completing the assignments and it upsets the heck out of me. I'm a history man! I want you to grasp why history is important!"

Mr. Elmo paused, looking at one student's face, then another's.

River frowned. Suddenly she remembered she had an overdue library book about Amelia Earhart.

She opened her desk.

"River?"

She quickly closed her desk.

"What's important about history?"

She shrugged.

"Well, you won't find out with your head stuck inside your desk. Recognize the importance of history: Know where we've come from. Know where we're going to. Let's not repeat the mistakes. Why else should we know history?"

Henry raised his hand.

"Can I go to the boys' room?"

"Yes!" said Mr. Elmo. He frowned. "And another thing . . ."

Another thing? River couldn't believe there could be another thing, after there had been this many things already.

"Several of you expressed frustration regarding the fact that Kirstin's name was picked out of the hat to spend a day at the junior high shadowing a junior-high student on Shadow Day. Grow up! Her name was chosen, fair and square. Stella picked her name out of my Orioles cap and you all saw it!" He began patting the top of his cap. "Right out of this baby!"

"Can you pat the top of your head and rub a circle on your stomach at the same time?" Henry asked politely as he picked up the bathroom pass.

"No!"

Brother. Can we get a little grumpier? thought River.

"Being *randomly* chosen for Shadow Day," Mr. Elmo said, "has simply nothing to do with the fact that Stella *randomly* picked Kirstin Walker's name for Student of the Month—nothing!"

Candace and River exchanged glances.

"Are you claiming my Orioles cap is rigged?" asked Mr. Elmo.

Nobody answered.

But everybody *was* beginning to question why Stella, whose classroom job assignment was to be Name Chooser, had magically picked Kirstin's name from the cap the last two times in a row.

The rumor was that Stella kept an extra folded piece of paper hidden between her fingers with Kirstin's name on it. When she reached into the cap she just slid that little folded piece of paper into the palm of her hand.

"Her family also won the raffle, though!" complained Margaret.

"Well, don't whine to me about it. You win some and you lose some. Some get rained out. *Honestly,* Margaret!"

Gosh! What's with Elmo, anyway? River wondered. Maybe his head did get too squeezed by his Orioles cap. Maybe his toes actually did get pinched.

Candace leaned across the aisle and whispered something to DB, who laughed out loud.

Mr. Elmo glared at him. "Something funny, Mr. Brand?"

DB shook his head no.

"Well, get with it," said Mr. Elmo. "All of you! Hop to it! What does it say on the schedule? 'Fractions Review'! I passed out worksheets on this a week ago. Where are they, lost in the rubble in your desks? Organization! Organization is the key! What are you waiting for, DB, Santa Claus? And stop tipping in that chair!"

The students leaned down and began poking through their desks.

Candace looked sideways at River, then scribbled a note on a small scrap of paper. She balled it up. Then she leaned down, pretended to fix her shoelace and rolled the note under River's desk.

River stepped on it and slid it under her chair

with her foot. She waited a moment, then leaned down and picked it up. She unwrapped it in her lap. Then she slyly looked down.

The note said: "The Elmomeister has PMS."

River smiled a little to herself.

Premenstrual syndrome—that was the problem! She passed the note forward. It made it all the way up one row of desks and halfway down another before it was intercepted by Kirstin Walker.

"Hey, I'm sorry," Kirstin said after reading it. "But I just have to say something: This is just so totally, like, immature. I mean, um, *some* kids may not be satisfied with the choice of me for Shadow Day, but then again a lot of people are."

She glanced at Stella and smiled.

"Personally, I'm getting sick of all the immature stuff, like this campaign *somebody* started. . . ."

She paused and made bug eyes at DB.

". . . altering the teacher's clothes," said Kirstin. "Make the cap too tight, make the boots too tight. *Oh, yawn.* And Mr. Elmo?" Kirstin walked to the front of the class. "I'm just not comfortable about this."

She let the note drop onto Mr. Elmo's desk.

"I feel like I need to say that some people in the class are so immature they feel they have to make jokes about stuff we learned in Human Interaction. It's like they can't handle it. I mean, like, grow up!"

She arched an eyebrow and looked in DB's direction.

DB stared at her.

"If I were you, Mr. Elmo, I'd give consequences for this. I mean, didn't we sign those pledges we wouldn't make fun of stuff we learned in Human Interaction class? Well, PMS is an actual problem for some women, and I find this note offensive. As a woman!"

River closed her eyes and sighed.

"Some of the kids in this room shouldn't be allowed to take Human Interaction," continued Kirstin, "because they're too immature to deal with the information."

She dogged Margaret.

"Thank you for sharing that with us, Kirstin. Sit down," said Mr. Elmo. He looked down and read the note. "This isn't funny, it's stupid. 'The Elmomeister has PMS.' That's supposed to be amusing?"

DB snorted.

"Who wrote this?"

Nobody answered.

"DB? Did you write this?"

With a crash, DB's chair tipped over backward and he fell on the floor. Mr. Elmo walked over. "I've told you a hundred times you'll hurt yourself. You okay?" He gave DB a hand up.

River watched as DB glanced around the room, silently making eye contact with his friends. He turned and looked past her at Henry and smiled, and River's heart fluttered a little in her chest.

She quickly looked down.

"I'm fine," said DB.

Brother! You can say that again, thought River. She snuck another peek at DB.

Yes, the Deebaroo was fine.

Most definitely.

Five

AT AFTERNOON RECESS, River called her mom again and arranged to be picked up a few minutes later so that she could make a more finished drawing of the idea she had for the border outside her classroom. The border would go around the doorway, above the windows, and over the arch above the drinking fountain.

The fact that DB was being kept after school in the classroom was purely coincidental.

River smiled a little, wicked smile.

Or was it?

She stood outside, looking at the wall and thinking and eavesdropping near an open window, listening to Mr. Elmo lecturing DB inside. "So, Mr.

Jokester," Mr. Elmo was saying, "you're lucky you didn't clobber your head tipping that chair. You think you're helping the class get the Class With Class Award with this type of nonsense?"

Maybe not, thought River. But she did think it was totally classy of DB to take the rap for writing the PMS note. She slyly peered into the room.

"And when you're done sweeping, get busy tidying this," Mr. Elmo was saying, "under here. What a darn mess!" He got down and began nesting some tin canisters in the cupboard under the sink, making clattering noises.

Suddenly Kirstin came huffing down the breezeway, making a desperate expression. "I can't believe it!" she called out to River. "I lost my mood ring!"

River pretended to care. "Really?"

DB poked his head out of the classroom doorway and made a pig nose at Kirstin as she approached. Then he closed the door in her face.

Kirstin rattled the doorknob.

She peered through the narrow window slot in the door. "Let me in!" she called.

River spied into the classroom again.

She saw DB smile, just a little, and turn his back. Then he began to loudly rearrange some tables.

River could hear Mr. Elmo complaining: "The faucet drips! The skylight drips! Look at that mess of a black tarp they've gone up on the roof and tried to cover the glass with. Darn it! They're getting me from above *and* below, doggone it! Look at this! Paintbrushes, paintbrushes, paintbrushes." He rattled the cans, his head in the cupboard.

River took a blue spiral notebook out of her pack. She stepped back and began drawing a picture of the exterior wall.

Kirstin walked over to River. "I can't believe it!" she said. "The butthead locked me out!"

"You're kidding!" said River without looking up. This was too good!

"Why would he do that?" said River.

"I *don't* know!" said Kirstin. She marched back over and booted the door.

Now DB was loudly putting the chairs up on the desktops.

River drew the doorway, the tile walls and the long bank of six windows that stretched along the wall. She drew two or three of the windows in the open position.

Kirstin booted and thumped on the door again. She swore under her breath.

River put in shadows on the left edges of the doorway and window frames. Then she walked very close to one of the open windows and pretended to examine the metal window frame. This put her in an excellent position for listening and spying.

"But where the heck's the paint?" Mr. Elmo was moaning as DB continued banging and clattering chairs.

Mr. Elmo poked his head farther inside the cupboard. "Everything's been cut out of the budget.

Next they'll be cutting out the rest room supplies in the teachers' bathroom. . . . What the heck are my geo boards doing under here?"

DB quickly stuck a times tables review tape into the tape deck and cranked up the volume. He loudly began singing along with a dorky review tune about the twelves.

Eventually Mr. Elmo heard Kirstin's howls and thumps. He walked over, swung open the door and kicked the doorstop down into place.

Kirstin hurried past him. "You jerk!" she called to DB, who was now dancing his way into the computer room.

River gently bit one finger to keep from smiling.

"I forgot my ring!" Kirstin said to Mr. Elmo. "And actually, it's my cousin's!" She lifted her desktop and began rummaging through it. "Where *is* it?"

"Looking for a mood ring?" said DB in a loud voice.

Kirstin whipped her head around.

"Well, what have we here?" said DB.

Kirstin watched hopefully as DB reached behind the computer.

He retrieved Mr. Elmo's Orioles cap.

"Mr. Elmo," he said, holding the cap in the air, "what shall I do with this?"

"Stick it where the sun don't shine," said Kirstin.

"I want you to leave my cap there, DB, exactly as you found it," said Mr. Elmo. "On the hook. By my jacket and my stadium boots. And turn down that tape!"

"Come *on*, Mr. Elmo!" called DB. He began making terrible disco moves. "Let's see you bust a move!"

River watched Kirstin storm over to the tape deck and turn it off.

"Thank God," said Mr. Elmo. "A little peace and quiet, that's all I ask." A drop of water fell from the ceiling and landed on his head. He looked up at the skylight. " 'Raindrops Keep Falling on My Head'—my new theme song," he said in a disgusted way. He dried his bald spot with his handkerchief. "But you tell 'em 'Don't put in skylights!' and do they listen? No, they put leaky plastic tarps on top of the glass, as if that will work. Darn it to heck!"

"I didn't find your hat exactly on the hook," said DB.

"Well, *so what!*" said Mr. Elmo, now really irritated about, well, everything. "Don't concern yourself with it! Is it computer-related? No. So you're not responsible for my hat or any other article of clothing or non–computer-related object in the computer area. As I said this afternoon, DB: Know *what* you're responsible for, *when*."

He walked over to his desk and began straightening it.

"And don't get any ideas about tightening that plastic hatband on me again. Did you tighten the band today?"

"Yes, sir."

"Well, don't change the notches again."

"I won't, sir, I promise you."

"Did you put paper in the toes of my stadium boots?" River heard Mr. Elmo ask. Her heart thumped.

"No, sir."

"Do you know who did?"

"Yes, sir."

"Do you know who sewed the ends of my jacket sleeves closed this afternoon?"

"Yes, sir."

"Well, tell her she snagged the lining," said Mr. Elmo.

"Why assume it was a girl, sir, just because sewing was involved?" said DB.

"Well, whatever the gender of the seamstress—or seamsperson," grumbled Mr. Elmo, "I wrenched my gol-dang wrist when it got stopped suddenly at the end of the sleeve." He rubbed his wrist. "And they snagged my darn jacket lining when I pulled the threads out!"

"Well, perhaps you should have clipped those threads more carefully, sir," said DB.

"No, I shouldn't have! And tell them to knock it off! Next time, there'll be consequences. I'm tired of the teasing," said Mr. Elmo. "Put the word out, would you, Deeb?"

"Okay," said DB.

"This old bird needs a break," said Mr. Elmo.

River began to draw again, peering over the top edge of her notebook. Now Kirstin was scouting the floor.

"Oh no!" Kirstin cried suddenly. She put her hand over her mouth. "I forgot! Stella borrowed my cousin's mood ring at lunch and didn't give it back! And my mother's makeup. And oh my gosh! She also borrowed the jacket I borrowed from my mother! Where's my mother's jacket and makeup that I borrowed without asking?"

Mr. Elmo picked up a yardstick from the blackboard tray and pointed to a rumpled pink jacket lying under a table near the cupboard where he kept the classroom balls and PE equipment.

"That jacket cost a fortune! Who stepped on it?" cried Kirstin. She crawled under the table and sat there for a moment, her head against the tabletop and her back against the ball cupboard door.

"Who stepped on this?" she said, lowering her eyelids to half-mast and peering suspiciously at DB, who looked back at her with a bored expression.

Kirstin sat under the table, clutching the jacket against her chest dramatically. "Who stepped all over my mother's jacket that costs eight dollars to dry-clean?" She looked in the jacket pockets. "And where's my mother's eyeliner and mascara?"

Mr. Elmo said nothing. He was busy balancing the yardstick on the palm of his hand. He walked a step forward, then a step back.

"DB, my homey," Mr. Elmo called, looking at the tip of the yardstick, "you've got a lot of poten-

tial—you're a bright kid, if you'd apply yourself."
He sidestepped to keep the yardstick straight.

River watched DB, who was watching Mr. Elmo
walk around his desk, balancing the yardstick. Suddenly Mr. Elmo lurched across the room toward the
doorway.

"And I know a smart kid when I see one—which
you are," said Mr. Elmo. "And don't forget it."

"I won't," said DB quietly.

"But I also know a kid who doesn't apply himself
when I see one, which you don't. You think you work
your hardest?"

"Nope."

"Well, I want you to try that. Good, better, best.
Never let it rest. Until the good is better. And the
better?"

"Best," said DB.

"Right," said Mr. Elmo. "*Now* watch!"

Mr. Elmo snatched the yardstick out of the air
and tipped his head way, way back and balanced the
yardstick vertically on the end of his nose.

"Watch the clock!" he shouted to DB. "Time
me!"

River stepped into the doorway. She and DB
watched the second hand sweep around the face—
ten seconds, twenty seconds, thirty seconds—

"—forty seconds, fifty seconds—"

"One minute!" called DB.

River glanced at Mr. Elmo and then back at the
clock.

"One minute ten," called DB.

"Twenty," called DB.

"Thirty," called DB.

After DB had called out two more minutes, Mr. Elmo let the yardstick drop into his hand.

"Not bad, Mr. Elmo," said DB.

Kirstin gathered her things and shoved her way past River and out of the classroom. "My mother's makeup *better* be on the ledge in the girls' room," she muttered as she hurried away.

Now River could see Mrs. Furley heading down the breezeway toward her.

"I could go longer," Mr. Elmo was telling DB, "but it makes my neck sore. I'm not as young as I used to be; things bother me more. My toe—it's painful as all get-out."

River felt a twinge of guilt.

"Anyway, I could go longer but it makes my neck sore and occasionally I get a crick in my neck when I'm not careful. But thank you, DB; I'm glad you're impressed. And I would like to point something out to you: I learned to do this when I was the same age as you. I practiced every day." He lowered his voice. "And I didn't get good at it by passing around notes about period menstrual signals," he added. "PMS. In my day, that was ladies' business. Now it's everybody's business!"

Mr. Elmo jumped. "Oh, hello, Mrs. Furley!"

Mrs. Furley was now standing beside River in the doorway.

"I didn't see you standing there!" said Mr. Elmo. "What can I do for you?"

"I left my demonstration supplies in the ball cupboard after the Pad Fest last week," Mrs. Furley explained. She shoved the table away from the ball cupboard, slid open the door and began taking out boxes and plastic bags with drawstring tops. "I need these at Longfellow School tomorrow."

River saw that DB and Mr. Elmo were making themselves very busy as Mrs. Furley stuffed the packages of overnights, slenders, megas, maxis, slims, winged and pantyliners into her canvas bag. "See you later," she said, tucking one last bag into her sack. The drawstring was open; a few pantyliners fell out. She stooped to pick them up. "Get in there, you guys!" she said cheerily to the pantyliners, shoving them back in and tightening the plastic string.

She waved goodbye to DB and Mr. Elmo.

They waved back.

Mrs. Furley waltzed out the door. On her way past River, she glanced at the drawing in River's notebook. "Looks good!" she said.

"Thanks," said River.

Mrs. Furley walked away. Inside the classroom, all was quiet. Mr. Elmo had moved to one side of the windows to untangle the cord of the draperies.

"Menstruation supplies in my ball cupboard," River heard him mumble to himself.

Suddenly River felt an overwhelming urge to rush into the room and give Mr. Elmo a hug—give a hug and a fat squeeze to the good old, funny old, big-beaked Elmo Dog.

Good old Mr. Elmo.

What would she ever do without him?

She felt sorry she had stuffed his boots with paper.

Sort of.

Six

RIVER SHOVED HER PENCIL into the spiral binding of her notebook. Her pack was resting against the wall by the door. She put her notebook into her pack. She lifted her pack onto one shoulder.

When she looked up, DB was looking at her.

"Bye, Deeb," said River.

"Bye," said DB.

Her heart fluttered.

"See you tomorrow," said DB.

"Yeah," said River.

"Bye, Mr. Elmo," River called. He was sitting at his desk. She decided to walk over to him and give him a pat on the back. "Hope those toes feel better," she said in a quiet voice.

"Let's see the drawing," said Mr. Elmo.

River took her binder back out and showed him.

Mr. Elmo whistled quietly. "Wow." He looked up at River.

"Thanks for taking the extra time to think about the school improvement project, River," he told her. "I can always depend on you. You're a very positive influence on all of us. I mean it."

"Thanks, Mr. Elmo," said River. "See ya."

Walking out, River felt deeply guilty . . .

. . . about leaving the Deebster behind.

But who told him to confess to a crime he hadn't committed? Candace would have admitted to writing the note, and when she did, River and Jules would have turned themselves in as coconspirators. And shared the blame and stayed after to straighten up.

Instead, the Deeb Boy had admitted to doing something he hadn't done. He took the rap for the girls, just the way Tom Sawyer did for Becky What's-Her-Name in that movie by Huckleberry Finn.

Or book or whatever it was.

River glanced back at the exterior wall of the classroom one last time.

A border, with a lot of color, maybe a Mexican motif, would do the trick.

If anything could push the class into first place for the first annual Class With Class Award, a colorful, flowered Mexican border brightening up the breezeway outside the room would do it. And maybe some huge paper flowers taped on the inside of the windows, facing out!

Just think: a group photo, a brass nameplate, a pizza party, no homework for a week, and best of all, an afternoon playing miniature golf in groups of six at Scandia: Candace and somebody, Jules and Henry, River and DB.

Mmmmmm. Mmmmm!

The perfect group. *Way* better than the limo group!

River walked to the front of the school. Kirstin's mother honked her car horn at River. "Where's Kirstin?"

"I think she went to the bathroom to try to find your makeup that Stella lost!" called River. She smiled innocently.

Now *that* was vicious, she told herself.

A moment later, Kirstin climbed into the front seat of the car and closed the door. She waved to River, then rolled down the window: "I'm serious," she shouted to River. "You honestly truly were my seventh choice for the limo party." She turned to her mother. "Wasn't she, Mommy?" she added in a loud voice.

Kirstin's mother looked over at River and made a face as if to say "Well, it wasn't *my* fault!" and then waved and drove away.

River's mother pulled up, and River hopped into the car and changed the radio station. Her mother pulled away from the curb; they passed Mrs. Furley in the lower lot, chatting with another teacher.

River's mother waved and Mrs. Furley waved back by swinging the large, square plastic bag she was holding by one corner.

"Gosh," muttered River. "What a nightmare!" She slumped down in the seat until her mother turned onto Adobe Road.

"What's a nightmare?"

"Furley," said River.

"Well, she's just doing her job," said River's mother. "I've heard she's an excellent teacher."

"Her job is to wave a bag of Stayfree Maxipad Overnights in the parking lot?"

"Is that what it was?"

River wiggled a little. "I've been in Wedgie Hell all day. Please don't pick out any more underwear for me. These even turned pink when I washed them!"

"I tip my hat to Mrs. Furley!" said River's mother. "She fought long and hard to develop the curriculum—"

"Did you hear me?" cried River. "I don't like these stupid underpants!"

"Good heavens, River! Calm down! And don't talk to me like that."

"Sorry," said River quietly. "But my undies bug me. And I need a nightgown that's less nipply. Hasn't Grandma figured out I'm not in kindergarten anymore?"

"*How* about starting by saying hello," said River's mother. "And asking me how I am."

"Hi, Mom."

"Hi, sweetheart."

"How are you?" said River.

"Miserable," said River's mother. "These ratty sale underpants aren't working out for me either. The leg holes seem to be the same size as the waist. Yesterday I wore them around all day without realizing they were on sideways. How was your day?"

"Fine," said River. "But I *do* need undies, a nightgown and lunch stuff. And Minnie Mouse napkins!"

"Well, we'll go to Ross. And Safeway. I'll pick up some chicken broth and noodles to make chicken soup for Megan," said River's mom. "She came home from school sick again today."

They drove along Adobe Road. River could see Henry ahead; he'd parked his bike and was on his hands and knees looking at something in the drainage ditch near the bike path.

"There's that nice Henry," said River's mother. "I bet he's looking for pollywogs."

"In February?" said River.

"Well, frogs, then."

River fixed her bangs a little. "He's probably waiting for DB—Deeb's helping Elmo clean up the room."

"Well, isn't that sweet of DB!" said River's mother. "He's always been such a considerate, helpful boy. When I was room mother, he always volunteered to eat all the extra cupcakes."

River sighed. "What's the matter with Megan?" She slyly looked sideways at Henry as they passed;

she watched him in the sideview mirror until they turned the corner. Henry was pretty cute. She could see why Jules liked him. But he wasn't as cute as DB.

"Megan has a queasy stomach again."

"What's a queasy stomach?" said River.

"Nauseated."

"Where do you get these words from?" said River.

"Pardon me! You don't say 'queasy stomach'?"

"Nobody says 'queasy stomach.' Not even Mr. Elmo says 'queasy stomach'!"

"At any rate, I think I'll make another appointment for Megan with Dr. Doyle."

River's mother began drumming her fingers on the steering wheel and softly singing along with the radio. " 'Do-wah-do-wah-do-wah-ditty,' " sang River's mom, " '—tawk about the boy from New Yawk City.' "

"Please stop!" River turned off the radio. "You're embarrassing me."

"Everything I do embarrasses you," said her mother. "My breathing air embarrasses you. I like music! I like to dance! People my age like to do a lot of stuff young people like to do!"

River's mother turned the radio back on, and River slouched down in her seat.

They pulled into the parking lot of Raley's Towne Centre. River's mother drove slowly past a coffee shop, looking for a parking space. "Ye Olde

Eggery!" mumbled River. "Who would want to eat breakfast in an old eggery?"

If River became a famous graphic artist and owned an advertising firm, anybody who suggested calling anyplace *ye olde* anything or who called any restaurant any kind of eggery, or eatery, or mug-duggery, was going to get the boot.

They parked and got out of the car.

"Mom?"

"What."

"Why do you keep wearing Dad's pants and shirts?"

"It's the new look for moms with generous buns."

River glanced around the parking lot to make sure nobody had heard and walked quickly away from her mother.

"Oversized!" her mother called as she headed toward Safeway. "You think you're the only ones who like to wear baggies? And big shirts?"

River ignored her.

"Rapper style!" called River's mom. She held out her shirttails.

Yikes!

River hurried toward Ross without looking back.

Seven

RIVER TOOK A DEEP BREATH as she walked into Ross. She loved the smell of new clothes! She made her way through the sections marked SWEATERS, SKIRTS, JACKETS, and MATERNITY CLOTHES. Ahead was the lingerie section. She could see the racks and racks of pretty bras. Above the racks were signs that boasted that the everyday prices were *so much less* than regular department store prices!

In fact, it was two-for-the-price-of-one on merry widow bras!

River eyeballed a black one.

Next year she'd go to the Renaissance Faire with Jules and Candace. They'd rent costumes and buy merry widow bras!

To prop those olde honkers right on up there!

With good olde velvet costumes with laces up the front and a few fat socks stuffed inside, the girls would be quite the merry widows! And River might look just like Henry's aunt.

With a little luck.

And a significant growth spurt.

River prowled through the rack of nylon peekaboo bikinis and thongs of all colors. Thongs. What good were thongs? They showed your entire rear except for one thin strip up the middle . . . the ultimate wedgie!

She took her time selecting six pairs of pastel cotton undies in ladies' size 5. On the opposite rack she saw a flannel nightgown cut like a long baseball shirt. She held it up by the hanger. It had pictures of brown bears in baseball uniforms happily catching balls with mitts or standing at the plate to bat. She threw it over her arm. It was practical and warm; she could talk her mom into it.

Where was her mom, anyway?

She gazed across the store. Nearby, a pretty young pregnant woman was talking to a rack of coats. "Get out of there," the woman was saying impatiently. "I mean it!" There was movement in the coats. "Okay, I'm going without you, then," said the woman.

"Okay, bye," said a tiny voice from inside the coatrack.

River saw her mother walk up to this woman.

Uh-oh!

Now her mother was going to start giving shopping advice.

To pregnant strangers!

She watched her mother move her reading glasses up onto her nose and check the tag on a hooded plaid maternity jacket. "Look at this," she heard her mother say in a loud voice. "Sixty-eight from a hundred and ninety-five."

She took it off the rack. "Nice fabric. Feel it!"

The young woman felt the fabric.

Good grief! Now she was making pregnant strangers pet maternity coats!

"But look, it's not that roomy," said River's mother. She held it up against herself, and the pregnant woman agreed.

Then, "Out!" said the woman to the coatrack again. "Where are you?"

"In fact," said River's mother, looking down at the jacket resting against her front, "it's downright skimpy." She put the jacket back.

Then she started hanger-banging through maternity outfits. "Why do you suppose they do this to us?" she said. She held up a pink-and-blue-checkered pants-and-top outfit with cap sleeves. "With two little lop-eared bunnies on the pocket . . . terrible! Do they think *we* turn into babies when we're having babies?" She hung the outfit back up. "When are you due?"

Gosh, Mom! Get a little nosier! thought River.

"Two weeks," said the woman.

"Well, congratulations," said River's mother.

"You're in the home stretch." The woman smiled a little bedraggled-looking smile, and River's mother parted the coats. "I'm the manager," she said in a stern voice. "Everybody out of the coatracks."

A small girl, with the face of an angel, emerged. Her perfect short, black bangs were lifted slightly by static electricity. She held on to her mother's leg and stared up at River's mother.

"Hi, Shorty!" said River's mother.

"Now, let me leave you with some good news," River's mother told the little girl's mother. "These shorties actually grow up and out of coatracks." She lowered her voice. "And into bras and high-heel shoes."

She glanced over her shoulder in River's direction.

River fiercely frowned at her.

"Soon you'll find yourself sitting on a pink upholstered chair at Victoria's Secret," she whispered, "with a pile of bras on your lap, waiting for your kid to get out of the dressing room!"

Now what's she talking about? thought River. She decided she'd better walk closer. "Of course," continued her mother, *"you'll* be wearing a pair of your husband's chino pants and a flannel shirt. And, if you've been robbed of as many pairs of underpants as I have, maybe even a pair of his briefs!"

My mother is a crazy person, thought River. "Hello!" she called. She held the nightshirt up to change the subject. "Can I get this?"

"Here's one of them now!" said River's mother. "My younger former coatrack inhabitant."

"Is she your grandma?" the little girl said to River.

River chuckled to herself. "Yes," she said, "she is."

"Say bye-bye," said the young woman to her daughter.

"What the . . . ," said River's mother when they were out of earshot. She caught a glimpse of herself in the mirror and moved a lock of gray hair away from her forehead. "Now I'm a grandma!"

They bought the nightgown and the underwear and left the store.

"I don't think it was very nice for you to call that little kid Shorty," said River as they drove out of the parking lot and headed home.

"Why not? She was a little shorty—a little sassy shorty squatty-body, just like you used to be.

"Yes, my dear," continued River's mother, remembering. "You, too, were a shorty squatty-body with thunder thighs. Michelin Man legs, we used to call 'em. *And* you had a rhumba rump."

"Stop saying that!"

River's mother smiled a small, wicked smile. "Sometimes the truth hurts."

"Like when that little girl thought you were a grandma?" said River. "You look great though, Mom, really!"

She stared at her mother's foot on the accelerator. "Where did you get the sandals?"

"You like them?"

"They're okay." River paused. "Mom?"

"What."

"You have a goat hair growing out of your chin."

Her mother sighed. "I'm a grandma with whiskers."

Eight

RIVER'S MOTHER CLATTERED into River's bedroom. "Are these shoes better than the sandals?"

"Mom! Where are you getting these things?"

"I've been cleaning out closets. Clogs are in style again."

"They are not," said River.

"Yes, they are; I saw them in Macy's."

Her mother lifted one leg and flexed her foot muscles so that the clog slapped against her heel a few times. "Which goes to show you: If you wait long enough to go through your closet, you'll be back in style."

She sat on the edge of River's bed.

"Your father bought these for me when I was pregnant with you so I wouldn't have to bend down and tie my shoes. Or, rather, so *he* wouldn't."

She flopped onto her back.

River sat and flopped beside her.

They lay there for a moment without talking.

"Furley's talking about being pregnant in sex class," said River.

"What does she say?" said River's mother.

"Are you taking things from the closet to the Salvation Army?" asked River, to change the subject.

"Yup."

"Well, I have that Grandma nightgown to give away once it's washed. And Mom?"

"What."

"Give the Salvation Army those sandals you had on."

"So anyway, what did Mrs. Furley say about being pregnant?" said River's mother.

"The minute I say anything about sex ed you always have to ask a million questions!" cried River.

"Well, I'm interested, and I'd like to remain involved with your schoolwork!"

"Then tell me ten outward signs of pregnancy. Henry's already come up with 'big honkers.' "

"He called them honkers?"

"Hooters, actually," said River.

"Well, that's rude. But anyway, there's also 'tender breasts.' And 'sleepy.' And 'morning sickness' . . . and *let* me tell you, I can say a thing or two about morning sickness! And, of course, there's always 'missed period.' "

"She already told us that."

"But you know what?" said River's mom. "When *I* was first pregnant, I didn't actually miss that first period. So I didn't realize I was pregnant! I spotted a little, so I assumed I was having a light period, which wasn't unusual for me."

Gosh! Not more spotting talk!

River rolled her eyes, but her mother ignored her.

"One Saturday afternoon, I took Megan with me and went into Safeway to get something for dinner. Megan, of course, was insisting on pushing the cart. She had talked me into animal crackers and had pitched two or three boxes of them into the little fold-out baby seat. I walked behind her as she wheeled the cart into a bread display and a number of customers, and eventually we reached the meat department."

River pretended to be bored.

"I took one look at a row of big, red slabs of raw rump roasts tied up in string and wrapped in plastic and suddenly I said to myself, '*Get* me out of here.' And I just grabbed Megan's hand and hurried out of the store, gagging.

"I drove home with Megan yelling about animal crackers. And I walked into the house and whispered to Daddy, 'Guess what? We're going to have another baby.'

"Dad jumped up and said, 'Are you sure?'"

"And of course I wasn't sure. So Dad drove straight to the drugstore and bought a pregnancy test kit. And stopped back by Safeway for the animal crackers—"

"Do you know how many times you've told me this story?" said River.

"No—how many?" said her mother.

"Go on," said River.

River heard Megan's door open and heard Megan go into the bathroom.

"I did the in-home pregnancy test."

River heard Megan cough in the bathroom; then she heard the toilet flush.

"Sweetheart?" called River's mother to Megan, but Megan didn't answer.

River's mother got up. She walked across the hall to the bathroom door. She leaned close to the crack. "Are you okay?"

Megan said nothing.

"Megan?"

"I'm fine!" shouted Megan.

River flinched.

"Leave me alone!" shouted Megan. "Can't I even go to the bathroom in peace?"

River followed her mother into the kitchen, where her mother was en route to the stove with six eggs in a pan of water.

"Was Dad happy?" River asked.

"Very happy," said her mother.

"Was Megan happy?" said River.

69

"I didn't tell her right away; I wanted to wait awhile, to make sure the pregnancy was going okay. I mentioned to you that I had a miscarriage once. . . . It was such a disappointment!"

Her mother stood staring at the pot full of eggs, remembering. "Anyway, seven months would have been such a long time for Megan to wait for a baby to arrive. She was happy to get the animal crackers, though," she added cheerily.

"Mom?" said River.

She watched as her mother adjusted the flame. "What."

"I think it's gross what people do to get a baby."

"Oh, you do, huh?"

"Yes! And I'm going to say I'm sick and stay home from school when Furley gets into the details! I mean it!"

"Well, you must admit it's a natural enough event. Look at that magnificent creature, in full bloom!"

River's mother pointed to Helene, who was petting herself by hunching her back and walking back and forth under the bottom rung of the kitchen chair.

"All creatures have their own unique and amazing courtships. Isn't she fabulous?"

River stared at Helene.

Helene stopped and stared back, her belly almost brushing the linoleum.

"Do you know how she accomplished that enormous gut?" said River's mother. "One enchanted evening, a tomcat with a tail like a broomstick and a face like a prizefighter jumped up on the windowsill and began serenading her. It woke me up. I got up and looked out the window. He glared at me and hissed."

"You're making this up," said River.

"A moment or two later, in the light of the silvery moon, I could see them 'getting acquainted' in my herb garden."

River stared at her mother for a long moment.

"Mom?" said River. "Don't ever make me pesto or rosemary chicken again."

Her mother leaned down and talked to Helene. "If you didn't want the responsibility of all these kittens, you should have postponed having sex."

Megan appeared in the doorway. "I don't think that's funny, Mom."

"Sorry. I was only kidding."

"Well, Helene's practically just a kitten herself!" said Megan. "You were supposed to get her neutered at the vet three months ago!"

"But the vet was in the Bahamas!"

"You could have taken her to the clinic," said Megan. "It was your responsibility."

"That's true, I guess," said her mother. "Want a soft-boiled egg?"

"Ick," said Megan.

"Want a hard-boiled egg in ten minutes?"

"Mom! Are you kidding? I told you my stomach's upset," said Megan.

"Sorry," said her mom. "I called from Safeway

and made an appointment for you to see Nancy Doyle—"

Megan looked at the ceiling. "I do *not* need to go to the doctor!" she cried. "There's a flu going around my school. I told you!"

"We're having boiled eggs for dinner?" said River. "What happened to the chicken soup?"

"I *hate* chicken soup!" said Megan.

"These are for egg salad sandwiches for tomorrow's lunches."

Megan sighed. "Is there *any* way I can convince you I don't want eggs? In any form?"

"Then I have a small roast I can cook and slice the leftovers for sandwiches. Megan, get it out of the refrigerator for me, will you?"

The phone rang.

Megan opened the refrigerator door.

Suddenly she closed the refrigerator door. "*You* get the meat out," she said to River, and hurried out of the room.

River took out the roast and put it on the counter. "Is this dead cow?"

"Yup."

"Did I tell you I'm a vegetarian?"

Her mother peered at her. "Not recently. Weren't we just at McDonald's last weekend?"

River said nothing.

Megan walked back in. "Mom? Could I take Anton to dinner in Chinatown for his birthday tomorrow? If he passes his test for his license?"

"On a school day?"

"*After* school!" said Megan.

Her mother frowned.

"It's his birthday. Please, Mom!" said Megan.

"Where will you two park?"

"In *Chinatown!*" cried Megan. "Hurry and decide! He's on the phone!"

Her mother arched an eyebrow at her. "I am *not* going to decide this in the next five seconds. But *if* I say yes, I want you two back in this house by ten o'clock."

"Will you pay?" asked Megan quietly.

"How much?"

"I don't know. About thirty bucks, I guess," said Megan.

Her mother sighed. "Clear it with your father when he calls tonight. He's never home to help me supervise you! Go to Chinatown with a boy who's had a license for one hour? I'm tired of making all the decisions! And what about your upset stomach?"

"It comes and goes," said Megan.

They looked at each other for a moment.

Then Megan looked down at the floor.

"Mom?" she said.

"What."

"What's with the clogs?" said Megan.

Nine

IN THE MORNING, River sat at the kitchen table, eating Cheerios from a coffee mug and listening to a Bob Marley CD.

Megan had riffled through the junk basket before she left for school, looking for a pen; her driving pamphlet had fallen on the floor. River picked it up. On the cover was a bad drawing of two happy-looking jerks in the front seat of a car. "Parent-Teen Training Aid" was printed in black letters and, below it, "State of California DMV."

River leafed through it—stopping at a picture of a guy making a hand signal out the window.

Boy! It was going to be great to drive someday!

She studied a picture of Car A and Car B as Car A was making a turn.

Stay in your own lane!

Megan had made some doodles around the picture—the MTV logo and a cat wearing a baseball cap. And in the margin she had scribbled:

Fm. Pln. Clc.—123 Thyme S.

"Fumm-a-plun-a-click . . . Fumm-a-plun-a-click . . . ," River sang in her head. She began tapping a kind of reggae rhythm on the booklet. "Fumm-a-plun-a-click . . ."

She tapped a circle around the drawing of the cat in the baseball hat. It looked a little bit like Mr. Elmo.

In his Orioles cap.

Hello, little Mr. Elmo Cat!

She tapped around Mr. Elmo Cat again, then tapped down the margin.

Watch out, Mr. Elmo Cat! Your stadium boots are too small!

Then she closed her eyes and really got into it: "One-a-two-a-three-a-Thyme . . . One-a-two-a-three-a-Thyme . . ."

She opened her eyes.

Yikes! What time was it?

"Hurry up!" she called to her mother, and picked up her lunch.

They walked to the corner, and River caught the bus to school.

She lugged her backpack up the steps of the bus and walked down the aisle toward an empty seat.

"Sit here," said Margaret. She scooted over.

"Okay, but I can't talk," said River. "I have homework to finish."

"Did you do the Tickler yet?" said Margaret.

"I started it, but I didn't finish. And I can't talk," said River. "I'm serious."

"Well, my cousin Helen helped me make up quite a list, including growing a whole big patch of more pubic hair in some cases."

River turned to Margaret and frowned. "Shhh!"

"My cousin Helen said her neighbor told her when she was pregnant she practically needed a Weed Eater to adjust her bikini line!"

River cringed.

"And she grew a hairy happy-trail from her belly button all the way down," said Margaret.

"Thank you for sharing," said River. "That's enough."

She unzipped her pack. She better not have left her sex ed notebook on the kitchen table!

"So I guess 'increased body hair in the southern regions of the body' might be one for your list," said Margaret.

"Okay!" said River. "If you promise to stop talking, I'll add it."

River found her notebook.

"My cousin Helen helped me with the wording of my list," said Margaret, "and she said Henry's hooter deal actually was true, but we put 'larger mammary glands.' "

River plowed through her pack, past empty gum wrappers and broken crayons, and found an erasable pen.

She added "increased body hair" to her signs-of-pregnancy list. Now she needed two more.

"My dad took me to the public library last week," said Margaret quietly. "He knows that since I don't have a mom I'll be needing to check out books on growing up—along with talking to Helen. And Mrs. Furley."

She slid a book out of her pack and held it against her chest. "For your eyes only," she said to River. She barely revealed the cover. "It's *Are You There God? It's Me, Margaret*," she whispered.

"Ah," said River.

"Judy Blume."

"Ah," said River.

"The librarian recommended it to me. Ever read it?"

"Yup. My big sister read it to me when I was eight."

"She *did*?"

Margaret leaned a little closer to River and whispered, "Have you started yet?"

River sighed deeply. What a question!

"I can't talk, Margaret—honestly," said River. "I'm just so stressed out about my homework."

Margaret patted River's shoulder. "Take a few deep breaths," she said.

"Right," said River.

"Just slow, deep breaths," said Margaret.

River slowly breathed in. Leave me alone! she thought. I'm begging you!

Margaret peered at River. "Would you like to hold my crystal?"

"No thanks."

"It's the best crystal," said Margaret. She took off her necklace, a pink crystal hanging from a thin silver chain. "My cousin Helen gave it to me."

Help! thought River. Margaret's gone New Age on us!

"It was her favorite one—totally incredible for helping pick out peaches . . ."

"Ah," said River. She looked at the list in front of her.

". . . and nectarines and other plant friends at the grocery store. But it also has other powers, like creative energy," said Margaret. She held the crystal so that it could swing over River's notebook paper. "See how it catches the light?"

"Mmm-hmmm," said River.

"Just let your creative energy flow," said Margaret.

"Okay," said River. Now begins the hippie talk, she thought. Help! I'm being held captive in the sixties!

She ignored the rainbows that swirled on the paper as best she could.

"Put down 'urge to nest,' " said Margaret.

"No!" said River. "Let me think of my own!"

"Well, 'urge to nest' is a good one," said Margaret.

"If you're a pregnant bird it might be," said River.

"Can birds get pregnant?" said Margaret.

River didn't answer. She neatly added "Unable to look at raw meat" to her list.

"I'm starving," mumbled Margaret. "I forgot to eat breakfast."

Did that require a response? River kept looking at her list.

"I can't hold this crystal anymore," said Margaret a few minutes later. "I'm so tired and hungry. You okay without it?"

"Ummm-hmmm."

"I'm going to visualize chow mein," said Margaret quietly. She put the crystal necklace back around her neck and closed her eyes.

Thank God, said River.

She reviewed her list. Oops! She'd forgotten to write "more sleepy than usual." So she wrote it and closed her notebook.

Then she took out her sketch of the exterior of the classroom and worked on it. She had difficulty getting the perspective right when she was drawing the alcove with the drinking fountain in it near her classroom. And she *really* had difficulty getting the perspective of the fountain right.

So she decided to draw a kid standing in the alcove, bending over and having a drink of water.

She worked on this drawing uninterrupted for thirty minutes, until the bus pulled onto Adobe Road and she could see the school. River tipped her head sideways and admired her work. She had to admit it: The drinking boy looked quite a bit like the Deebster.

What a coincidence!

She smiled to herself and put her things away.

Margaret had fallen asleep.

River felt a little motherly, looking down at Margaret, snoozing with her head against the window. And she felt a little sad, knowing that Margaret didn't have a mom. That was probably why Margaret was hungry: no mom to hound her about Cheerios and juice.

And a vitamin pill.

"Wake up!" she said gently. She nudged Margaret.

They walked quietly to class. River still felt sad and sorry for Margaret—that Margaret's mom had died when she was just a baby, and that Margaret didn't have a big sister to show her the ropes. And leave pads hanging around in the cupboard for inspection and trial runs.

And she didn't have a sister to read her a Judy Blume book about a girl and God. River hated to think how long it might be before Margaret's prayers would be answered.

"By the way, I haven't," River told Margaret suddenly.

"Haven't what?"

River looked at her.

"Oh, *good*," said Margaret. "Me either.

"I don't even have one hair!" whispered Margaret.

River softly elbowed her to be quiet. All she needed was a boy to walk past with Margaret spilling her guts about periods and pubic hair. They walked down the breezeway toward the classroom without speaking.

Mr. Elmo was standing in the classroom doorway talking to Mrs. McPhearson. He had already gone through his morning routine: unzipping his stadium boots and putting on his moccasins, placing his stadium boots side by side on the floor, then taking off his blazer and hanging it carefully on a plastic hanger on a hook in the computer room—a ritual he might have learned from Mr. Rogers on TV.

"Here's our class artiste!" Mr. Elmo called when he saw River. "Show Mrs. McPhearson your breezeway plan!"

River set down her pack and took out her drawing.

"Look at this!" Mr. Elmo said to Mrs. McPhearson. "Would you?"

And they both stood there, admiring River's work.

River had drawn and colored in her proposed border: black, with colorful flowers, that ran along the windows and into the alcove and back out again.

River picked up her pack and went into the classroom. Margaret gave River's arm a squeeze as they parted. "Thanks, Riv," she whispered before going to her desk and sitting down.

"Someone's made a hat size adjustment," was all that Candace said to River as soon as River walked in. "Check it out. Elmo's Orioles cap! Quick! Before the bell rings."

River glanced out the doorway at Mr. Elmo, still chatting with the principal and admiring the artwork.

River walked backward down the aisle, still watching them. She turned and ducked into the computer room. She looked sideways at the Orioles cap, hanging from the hook by its plastic adjustable band.

DB casually walked past the doorway and frowned at River and mouthed the words: "Look *in* it! *In* it!"

River gently lifted the cap away from the wall with one finger and peered inside, but the hat tipped too far on the hook and fell off, landing upside down. She quickly picked it up by the bill and replaced it.

And hurried back to her seat.

Good heavens!

River quickly glanced at Jules and Candace.

The bell rang and Mr. Elmo led the Pledge of Allegiance.

As soon as everybody sat down, River heard a squeak and a snort. She turned around and saw Peter covering his mouth and nose with his hand.

"Pass these back to Peter," said Mr. Elmo, handing Noah a box of tissues. "Are you okay, Pete?"

Peter nodded.

Then Mr. Elmo opened his desk drawer and pulled out a colorful hat made of traditional African fabric. "Today," he announced, "as we near the completion of Black History Month, and in honor of the four hundred years of African American contributions to these great United States, I'm wearing this hat." He put it on. "Instead of my Orioles cap."

Mr. Elmo took time to place the cap correctly on his head. "There.

"My wife bought it for me at the Festival of the Lake last summer," he said. He gave the class a front, side, and back view, and River had to admit, it did look pretty good on him.

He looked at the class with a serious expression; soon it was absolutely quiet in the room. "I don't know how many of you know this," said Mr. Elmo, "but I was in Korea at the same time as a man by the name of Jesse Leroy Brown—the first African American to wear Navy wings. Don't ever forget that name.

"He received the Distinguished Flying Cross posthumously."

He paused.

Then he looked down at the floor.

"One of the biggest regrets of my life is that I didn't have the opportunity to fly with him."

River thought for a minute that Mr. Elmo's eyes got a little misty.

And it made her heart swell with pride to have a teacher who wasn't afraid to cry a little, remembering a fallen comrade, a hero, such as Jesse Leroy Brown.

Mr. Elmo took a beautiful piece of kente cloth out of a plastic Ziploc bag and hung it carefully on a hook near the flag. "The kente cloth will remain near the flag for the rest of the year," said Mr. Elmo. "As a reminder that Black History is American history and is not limited to the month of February."

Then he stood back and saluted the flag.

The class was quiet as Mr. Elmo took attendance.

And River thought that even though the class must now suddenly have become ineligible for the Class With Class Award, surely Mr. Elmo was the classiest teacher of any teacher in the world.

Ten

GIVEN THE NUMBER of students who now knew about the hat trick, and given that every student signed a pledge not to fool around about stuff related to Human Interaction class, and given the fact that every last student who knew about the trick continued to dishonor this pledge by sitting in Sustained Silent Reading daydreaming about the moment when Mr. Elmo would discover the latest alteration to his clothing, River had a question:

Should the class still even be considered for the Class With Class contest?

You had to wonder.

And so would the adult evaluators wonder, if they knew what she knew!

River decided not to think about it.

She put her nose in her book again.

Certainly Mr. Elmo would take points off for this.

Many points!

The question was: Should she, herself, make an excuse to go back to the computer room, sneak the cap off the peg, and do what she had to do to save the Class With Class Award?

She glanced at DB.

Was he the one who had thought up this fabulous prank?

Should she be the one to spoil the fun?

River read the same sentence over and over again, losing the meaning of the words four or five more times. Who had 'mounted the wild-eyed horses'? The good guys or the bad guys?

"Excuse me, Mr. Elmo," said a voice, and River jumped. Mrs. McPhearson was standing in the doorway! "I hate to bother you, but did I leave my clip-on sunglasses here? I've misplaced them somewhere over the past few days."

Mr. Elmo opened his eyes and began poking through some papers on his desk. "I don't think so."

"Rats!" said Mrs. McPhearson. "I promised the fourth-graders I'd be honorary referee for the volleyball playoffs this morning. When it's so bright out, it's hard to watch the ball." She looked at her watch. "I should be out there right now. The superintendent said he'd try to stop by."

"Really?" said Mr. Elmo.

"Yes, I'm hoping to interest him in initiating an after-school sports program, since the Human Interaction pilot program has gone so well here at Franklin."

She addressed the class: "And let me take another opportunity to congratulate all of you once again for your outstanding response to Mrs. Furley and your mature attitude toward her class. I just can't say how proud you've made us."

"No one's seen Mrs. McPhearson's shades?" said Mr. Elmo.

Nobody had.

"You're an example for the entire district!" added Mrs. McPhearson. "I tip my hat to you—or I would, if I had a hat!"

"Well, we can solve that," said Mr. Elmo. He stood up. To River's horror, and to the horror of the rest of the students who had been aching for the moment when Mr. Elmo found his great new disposable sweatband, he said to Mrs. McPhearson, "Why don't you borrow my Orioles cap?" and headed toward the computer room. "It will shade your eyes."

"No!" said Mrs. McPhearson. "I'll be fine."

"You sure?"

"Yes!" said Mrs. McPhearson. "I'm a Cardinals fan."

Yes, she's sure! River cried out to herself.

"I insist!" said Mr. Elmo.

She doesn't want to wear your stupid hat! thought River. Get a clue!

Mrs. McPhearson glanced again at her watch. Then she looked out the windows that faced onto the west yard. "Good grief! They're already out there waiting."

River turned and looked out onto the yard. The fourth-graders were taking their positions on the volleyball court.

Several students, including DB, began nervously copying math problems from the board onto a piece of scratch paper. A couple of boys who had been looking at magazines quickly took paperback books out of their desks and began pretending to read them.

Suddenly Margaret piped up with, "Wait a minute! What if Mr. Elmo has lice? I thought that paper you had us bring home in third grade said we shouldn't share hats! That head lice can be spread by sharing hats, scarves, combs and brushes! Remember? In that bulletin a couple years ago?"

Thank you, Margaret Rothrock! said River to herself.

"That was sent to all the schools in the district from the superintendent's office?" said Margaret. "You *must* remember!"

Keep at it, Margaret. Don't let up . . .

"Or was it the district nurse?" said Margaret. "Maybe it was from Mrs. Furley! Didn't she used to be the district nurse?"

"Well, the hat warning wouldn't apply in this situation," said Mrs. McPhearson.

"Why not?" cried Margaret. "It should apply in every situation!"

Mrs. McPhearson looked at Margaret. "Think about it," she said in a quiet voice.

Mr. Elmo turned around. "What?"

"Nothing," said Mrs. McPhearson.

"Lice can too lay eggs on that head!" whispered Margaret. "In the fringe, in the back! Or in that little swoop of hair up on top!"

Mrs. McPhearson put her finger on her mouth and frowned at Margaret. She folded her arms on her chest and looked up at the ceiling. "Look at those water marks," she said. "That skylight really does need to be fixed."

Mr. Elmo walked into the computer room. "Where are you?" he called to the Orioles cap. "Ah!" He grabbed it off the peg and tossed it into the air so that it made a few vertical revolutions before he caught it again by the brim. This maneuver answered any questions River might have had about the effectiveness of the adhesive strip on the back of a pantyliner.

Her heart began to thump.

Holding the cap behind his back as if it were a bouquet of flowers, Mr. Elmo walked up to Mrs. McPhearson and bowed. "Madam?" he said.

It's over, thought River.

He held it out to her by the brim.

It's all over, thought River. The pizza party's over, the miniature golf is over. . . .

Cancel the group photographer. . . .

Mrs. McPhearson took the cap by the bill, grabbed the plastic band with her other hand, turned her head to the side, and put the cap on, without looking in it. She pulled the bill down over her nose. "It's a little snug," she mumbled. "But it will do."

Mr. Elmo smiled broadly at the class. "It looks terrific on her, doesn't it, people?" A few kids nodded. "Maybe she'll end up switching teams!"

"I *doubt* that," mumbled Mrs. McPhearson. She headed out the door.

"Now. Where were we?" said Mr. Elmo.

The entire class sat without speaking.

Except Peter. "Good heavens, Peter!" said Mr. Elmo. "What's going on?"

Peter had begun to laugh. He waved his book in the air above his head. "The book!" he gasped. "It's a riot! You've *got* to read it!" He gathered himself, but only for one moment.

"Really!" he told Mr. Elmo. "It's hysterical!" Then he chucked the book into his desk and fell apart, covering his face and howling into his hands.

"What book is it?" said Mr. Elmo.

"*Where the Red Fern Grows*," Peter moaned in a muffled voice.

River closed her eyes and shook her head.

Where the Red Fern Grows: the saddest book she'd ever read in her life.

Eleven

"BACK TO BUSINESS," said Mr. Elmo, taking off his glasses and folding them up in preparation for a Sustained Silent Catnap. River peered at Candace, who was smiling behind a book she was holding in front of her face.

"It isn't funny!" whispered River.

"Yes it is!" said Candace.

"I said, back to business," said Mr. Elmo to River.

River began to read about the horses again, but within a few seconds she found herself reflecting on the source of the class's collective guilt.

And she wondered, yet one more time, how the ninety percent of parents and teachers who had pushed for the Human Interaction program would feel at this moment if they knew what River and her classmates knew as they tried not to watch Mrs. McPhearson, standing in the distance in a blue suit and sensible shoes, whistle in her mouth, refereeing the volleyball game.

With a pantyliner stuck in her cap.

Read! River told herself.

Where was she? ". . . and they galloped across the desert, the horses wild-eyed—nostrils flared, foaming and frothing at the bit . . ."

Horse spit.

Yuck!

Who would put horse spit in a book?

Who was this author? Didn't he have an editor?

River gazed past the top of the page, through the window, past the temporary buildings. And wondered, What if the Orioles cap fell off and landed upside down on the asphalt during the game? It would lie there, like a turtle unable to right itself, helplessly exposing its private under-shell to a group of fourth-graders. And they would see a pantyliner—an innocent group of ten-year-olds would see a pantyliner and wonder what it was.

I didn't do it! she cried out to herself.

But you knew about it, a small voice said within her. You could have taken it out! You could have thrown it away.

"Gosh!" River whispered to Candace. "I hope the hat doesn't fall off!"

Candace looked out the window for a few seconds. "Really?" she said. "Why?"

River frowned at her. "The little kids will see it," she whispered, "and wonder what it is!"

"They've never been in a grocery store before?" whispered Candace.

River thought a minute. This was a comforting thought, realizing that the kids in the volleyball tournament must have, at one time or another, wheeled the family grocery cart past boxes of pantyliners sitting brazenly on grocery shelves.

"It would embarrass Mrs. McPhearson!" whispered River.

Candace smiled a wicked little smile. Mr. Elmo opened one eye and looked at her.

"And it's gender harassment!" whispered River.

Candace stopped smiling. "It *is?*"

"Our whole class will get in trouble!" whispered River when Mr. Elmo closed his eye again.

Soon River felt Jules gently nudging her.

Jules handed River a note.

River read it. She folded it up and put it in her pocket. Yes, she supposed there was some logic in what Jules had written; Mrs. McPhearson had a lot of training and experience.

But wasn't this experience just *a little* beyond the scope of a Ph.D. in elementary education?

She peered out the window again.

Oh.

My.

Gosh.

Two men in suits had appeared! They were standing on the sidelines of the game with their arms crossed on their chests. They looked like FBI agents; but FBI agents would have no reason to be surveilling a volleyball game at Franklin Elementary. . . .

Unless they were investigating the theft of a pantyliner! Were the demonstration Pad Fest pads state property?

You're losing your mind! River told herself. The FBI wouldn't put two agents on the Case of the Missing Pantyliner! The guys in the shades must have come from the superintendent's office.

River glanced at Mr. Elmo. He had now nodded off. Sweet dreams! thought River. And let him not be awakened by the principal, the superintendent and—who could the other guy be?

Read! thought River. She peered over the top of her book again. It shouldn't be long before the game was over, she thought, and it wasn't.

A few minutes later, she saw the three of them stroll past the windows that opened up onto the breezeway. They stopped for a short time; Mrs. McPhearson, still wearing the Orioles cap, pointed through the glass at the ceiling of River's classroom. Then they continued.

Now what?

River leafed through her book. Mr. Elmo let out a little snortish snore, and her heart leaped in her chest.

A student messenger appeared at the door. "River?"

River looked up.

The messenger tiptoed past Mr. Elmo and handed River a note.

"Please come to the office," was written on a memo from Mrs. McPhearson's desk. River put her hand on her chest.

She looked up at Candace and then Jules.

She looked at DB.

They stared back at her with worried expressions.

River quickly got up. She hurried down the breezeway.

Why was she being called to the office?

She wasn't the only one who knew!

Just about everybody knew about the hat trick—except for Kirstin.

And Stella.

And the rest of the limo group.

She heard her footsteps. She heard herself breathing.

Kirstin was right: The class wasn't mature, or ma-toor, or whatever you called it, like Mrs. McPhearson thought. They were just a bunch of sixth-graders who lacked integrity and as a consequence weren't going to play miniature golf or eat pizza—with or without pepperoni.

They were just a bunch of ungrown-up brats. The Human Interaction class should be canceled;

plus, they should have a hundred points subtracted from their Class With Class score. At least!

Mrs. McPhearson was sitting at her desk with the door open when River walked into the office. "River?" she said. "Come in."

River walked quietly in.

"The superintendent and his assistant were just here," she began.

River looked at the floor.

". . . and I told them about your plan for a border for the breezeway outside your classroom. The superintendent said he would entertain the possibility of sending over paint and two district painters to implement your design, and extend it."

"To *what*?" said River.

"To use your design pattern and paint the border along the exterior walls of all of the classrooms to pep the breezeways up. What would you think of submitting your design?"

"I would submit my design for that," said River. She looked up.

"And River? I must say you have an extraordinary talent."

"Thank you," said River.

"Good," said Mrs. McPhearson. "We'll be in touch, then."

"Okay!" said River. She paused, her heart thumping. "And Mrs. McPhearson?"

"Yes?"

River walked up very close to Mrs. McPhearson and asked, "Are you done with that cap?"

"As a matter of fact," said Mrs. McPhearson, "I am." She closed her eyes and took it off, pressing her fingers to the middle of her forehead. "It's so tight, it's giving me a headache."

"That's too bad!" cried River, grabbing the cap from Mrs. McPhearson's hand and putting it on her own head.

Mrs. McPhearson opened her eyes. "Watch out for nits," she whispered with a sly grin.

"I will!" cried River. She hurried down the hall toward the trash can outside the cafeteria door. The coast was clear.

She started to take off the cap but was startled by the custodian, who suddenly wheeled her mop and bucket out the double doors.

River continued down the breezeway.

The music teacher passed. The PTA president passed! What was this, a parade?

She was almost at her classroom!

Where could she ditch the pantyliner?

Suddenly she heard Kirstin's voice in the doorway of the classroom.

Then she heard Mr. Elmo say, "This couldn't wait?"

River ducked into the alcove and plastered herself between the fountain and the wall. She heard what Kirstin and Mr. Elmo were saying as they walked out of the classroom and took a few steps down the breezeway.

"Four more minutes, Kirstin, and SSR would have been over," grumbled Mr. Elmo. "You couldn't have waited?"

"Actually, not really," said Kirstin.

"I think you'd better retrieve your hat from Mrs. McPhearson," she said in a low voice. "Don't say I said so, but I think River and DB did something to it, in violation of the Human Interaction pledge, after school yesterday."

River's stomach dipped. She slowly reached up and eased the cap off her head and tucked it under her arm.

"I would have warned you earlier, I swear it," Kirstin said, "but I just found out two seconds ago."

Mr. Elmo looked up as though gathering his thoughts. "Kirstin," he began after a moment had passed, "Kirstin, Kirstin, Kirstin. What are you trying to do here? You stuck that what's-it-called in my hat after school."

Kirstin pointed to her chest. "Me?"

"Yes, you."

"I did *not!*"

"Yes you *did.* I saw your reflection in the skylight when I was showing DB my balancing trick. The skylight is covered with black tarpaper on the outside; this causes a mirror effect."

River's eyes grew rounder. Kirstin? Getting *busted?* This was too good to be true!

Mr. Elmo suddenly looked at the doorway of the classroom. "Margaret!" he said sternly. "I will *not* tolerate an eavesdropper! I know you're listening!"

Margaret appeared in the doorway. "I am not." She disappeared again.

River tried to make herself smaller.

"*You* snuck it out of Mrs. Furley's festival supplies that she had stored in my ball closet!" Mr. Elmo was saying to Kirstin. "*You* tiptoed into the computer room and stuck it in my cap because *you* wanted to set up River and DB. Are you aware that I worked in law enforcement after I got out of the service? As an investigator?"

"Now how would I know that?"

"Well, I did," said Mr. Elmo.

"Do I care?" said Kirstin under her breath.

"Now, go back into the classroom and have a seat," said Mr. Elmo.

"It was just a joke, for Pete's sake!" said Kirstin. "Everybody's so serious around here! It was a joke. So big deal."

"A joke, under appropriate circumstances," said Mr. Elmo, "like at an all-gal pajama party, a Q-tex pad in a hat may be a joke—"

"A Q-tex pad?" said Kirstin.

"Well, whatever the brand is!" said Mr. Elmo. "Myself, I don't buy the darn things. That's my wife's department, or was. In any event, in the context of a classroom, this 'joke' is nothing more than a form of harassment, an act of disrespect and immaturity for which there will be consequences."

Mr. Elmo glanced at the doorway again. "Margaret!" he shouted. "I mean it!"

River heard footsteps; a chair clattered. She peeked out from the alcove.

"So of course I removed that darn thing and put it in my blazer pocket before I gave the cap to the principal."

Mr. Elmo walked solemnly to the classroom. Kirstin followed him.

"We need to select another student to represent the class on Shadow Day at the junior high," Mr. Elmo announced from the doorway. "Kirstin will be too busy that day working on a science report on mirrors I plan to assign to her and her only. Fascinating how mirrors work!"

River looked inside the baseball cap. It was empty except for a tag marked OFFICIAL something. She took a moment to curve the bill a little better; then she put on the cap, pulled the bill down low over her eyes, and walked down the breezeway to her classroom.

She squeezed past Mr. Elmo and Kirstin, and the class breathed a collective sigh of relief.

"But I'll tell you something," Mr. Elmo was saying to Kirstin, "mirrors don't work by putting tarpaper over a skylight. You took the bait, hook, line and sinker. You were simply a suspect; now you've confessed."

"Just wait a minute here," said Margaret. "You didn't read Kirstin her rights!"

"This is a classroom, not a police station. She's not entitled to a lawyer!" said Mr. Elmo.

"You still should have warned her," said Margaret.

"About what? I'm not a cop," said Mr. Elmo.

"Well, you just said you worked as a law enforcement officer once!" said Margaret.

"In *any event*," shouted Mr. Elmo, "I'm relieving Kirstin of her post as representative of our class on Shadow Day at the junior high."

He turned to Kirstin: "*Not* because of the ridiculous prank which violated the pledge you seemed so committed to, but because you tried to set up and frame two other students."

Everybody in the class just sat there without speaking, gazing at him. Good old, sturdy old, stouthearted Mr. Elmo with his big gut, prominent nose, bald head, and glasses taped with adhesive tape.

What a guy!

Kirstin went back to her seat, walking lightly on her feet as if none of this mattered. She sat down with a self-satisfied look and glanced around the room to find support among the first six kids she had thought of inviting to her limo party.

"And now we'll need another Shadow Day student. But, this time I think we'll open it up to the democratic process. Any nominations?" Mr. Elmo tossed a small piece of chalk into the air and caught it.

Margaret shyly raised her hand. "Mr. Elmo?"

"Yes, Margaret?"

"Can we see you do your yardstick balancing act?"

"I nominate Margaret Rothrock for Shadow Day," said River, peering out from under the cap's brim.

"I second the nomination," said DB.

"All in favor?" said Mr. Elmo.

"Aye!" shouted almost everybody.

"Opposed?"

"Nay!" shouted the limo party.

"Ayes win. You're on your way!" Mr. Elmo said to Margaret.

Margaret stood there with her hand on her chest. "Me?" Her eyes filled with tears. "The class elects *me* to go to the junior high?"

Mr. Elmo grabbed his yardstick, threw it in the air, whirled in a circle and caught it before it hit the ground. He stood frozen, gazing at Margaret with eyes like blue ice.

"Yes, Margaret," he said. "You're the chosen one."

"Now!" he said, tipping his head way, way back and balancing the yardstick on the end of his generous beak. *"Time me!"*

Twelve

MR. ELMO DEDUCTED twenty-five points from the class score.

But River had to admit it: They all deserved it.

She could only hope that her border idea would put them back into the running.

So she very, *very* carefully and sneakily was drawing on a narrow strip of paper. Hidden in her Human Interaction binder.

River's plan was to submit two alternate designs, in addition to her original: one roses-on-a-China-blue background, one morning-glories-on-a-hot-pink background.

But she'd better hurry up!

The contest would be over soon!

She could hear Mrs. Furley talking to the class.

She looked up every once in a while, with her usual captivated expression.

Maybe River shouldn't have been drawing—but along with drawing on the strip, she was going to make *excellent, completely complete notes.*

And earlier, the class had agreed: There would be *no more foolaround* in sex class—Human Interaction class, rather.

A lot of the kids had already completely shaped up; many were actually answering Mrs. Furley's questions voluntarily.

"Mmm-hmmm," Mrs. Furley was saying, "a person could go to a doctor's office to talk about questions he or she might have about birth control or pregnancy counseling. And where else?"

River glanced around the room.

Gosh!

Now Henry was even raising his hand.

"Could I get a drink of water?" Henry asked.

Mrs. Furley nodded.

"Well, how about the county health department?" said Mrs. Furley. She turned around and added "county health department" to the list she had already begun on the chalkboard. "And has anyone heard of Planned Parenthood? Planned Parenthood is an example of a family planning clinic." She wrote "family planning clinic" and underlined it.

River wrote "cty. hlth. dept." at the bottom of the list she was copying from the board.

Then she added "fm. pln. clc."

And stared at it.

Where had she seen this before?

Fm. pln. clc. . . .

Suddenly River's skin felt prickly. Her heart began to race. Why was "Fm. Pln. Clc." written in Megan's driver's guide?

Why would Megan have written "Fm. Pln. Clc." and the address of the family planning clinic in the margin?

An odd, sad, sinking feeling came over River; she took a breath, but she felt as if she couldn't get over the top of it, couldn't fill her lungs with air.

"Planned Parenthood is actually the most well known of the clinics. It's a national organization," Mrs. Furley was saying.

So that was it.

Megan was pregnant.

River put her pencil down.

Megan was pregnant. That was why she had an upset stomach. That was why she kept racing into the bathroom: to throw up! That was why she had been falling asleep instead of doing her geometry homework. That was why she had run away from the rump roast in the refrigerator!

Calm down, River told herself. You don't know this for sure.

But River *did* know this for sure. Megan was pregnant and, someplace, deep down in, River had known it all along. It had been like a shadow in the back of her mind.

She tried to breathe normally but couldn't seem to catch her breath. She just sat there, looking at the paper in front of her.

"River?" said Mrs. Furley, putting a worksheet on top of River's notebook. "How are you doing?"

"Good," lied River.

She felt empty and sick, as if she might throw up if she tried to eat her lunch.

Lunch.

What a terrible thought!

She stared at the worksheet.

It said:

OPTIONS FOR A PREGNANT TEENAGER

1. *have the baby and raise the baby with help from family members;*
2. *have the baby and, with the help of an appropriate government agency, arrange for foster care until able to raise the child herself;*
3. *have the baby and, with the help of qualified adults, arrange for a legal adoption of the baby into an adoptive home;*
4. *end the pregnancy by arranging for a legal abortion performed in a medical facility by a doctor.*

River read the list again.

Megan pregnant, before she even got her driver's license! What would their father say?

She glanced at the clock.

His plane had probably already taken off out of

the airport in Reno. In fact, it had already probably landed in Oakland! He was probably driving home right now, driving in the Taurus, with a tape of symphony music playing, on his way home, and on his way to becoming a grandfather!

He was already upset enough about his bald spot and the gray in his beard! What would he say to Megan when he found out?

What would he say to Anton?

Why was he always out on the desert? It was his fault this had happened! He was out on the desert, instead of being at home to discourage teenage sexual activity with a partner. A respectful boy like Anton wouldn't have had the nerve to have sex with Megan if he'd known her father was sitting at home in a La-Z-Boy chair with the lamp on! Waiting for them to be home by midnight the way a father should have been, dozing. Instead of hanging out with a bunch of crazed Canadians and horny toads!

River decided she would tell her dad off once and for all the minute she walked through the door.

If he was home.

If he hadn't ducked out to his office for a few minutes—which would translate into a few hours. Then he'd be late for his meeting with her mom, and she'd be furious, and there'd be a divorce!

Maybe their meeting was *with* a divorce lawyer!

River's heart seemed to be jumping around in her chest now. *Get* a grip, she told herself. Calm down and think this through.

This is not your dad's fault, she told herself.

He has to make a living, doesn't he?

Her thoughts strayed to her mother. Did her mother know Megan was pregnant? Was this their little secret? Was this why she was so interested in maternity clothes at Ross? River began to feel light-headed.

"Mrs. Furley?" said Margaret quietly. "*When* are we getting our Brain Tickler lists back?"

"You just turned them in," said Mrs. Furley. "Why?"

"Because I want to know how me and my cousin did, that's why!" said Margaret. "I never seem to know how I'm doing in this class! And I'm the only one who never seems to know what's going on!"

"Margaret?" said Mrs. Furley. "I did happen to glance over your list, and you did a wonderful job."

"Oh," said Margaret in a tired way. "Well, I hope so," she said. "I'm the class representative for Shadow Day at the junior high, and I want to know everything there is to know about Human Interaction so I won't be considered an immature dope."

"Well, there's a lot of ground to cover here; you're not supposed to know everything all at once. You're doing fine, Margaret. Really!"

Margaret sighed. She reached up and clutched her crystal necklace and closed her eyes.

"Now what," said Mrs. Furley.

"I'm calming myself," said Margaret. "Reading

the paper you handed us makes me feel weird. I'm sick of this pregnant stuff; it stresses me out."

Yes, the list did seem kind of weird. Especially the last choice. And thinking about it made River feel a little sick; she felt sick and her arms and legs felt tingly and numb. Breathe! River said to herself.

She took two deep breaths. Then she did something she'd never done in Human Interaction: She raised her hand.

"Mrs. Furley?" she asked quietly.

"Yes, River?"

"What kind of counseling would a family planning clinic give?"

"Well, the counselors help the teen think things through, to see which decision might be best."

Margaret began waving her hand in the air again.

"Could a pregnant teen bring someone along?" said River. "Like her boyfriend?"

Mrs. Furley nodded.

"Oh," said River.

"Mrs. Furley!" said Margaret.

"Yes, Margaret!"

"I'm wondering. Is today really going to be the end of this?"

"Of what?" said Mrs. Furley.

"I mean—according to the course outline, next week—it's boys' you-know-whats. Right?" said Margaret.

Mrs. Furley began checking her notes. "Is that what it says?" She eyeballed her outline. "Hmmm, I guess it does. We'll wind up pregnancy and move on. Okay?"

"*Yes!*" said Margaret in a whisper.

Thirteen

DB AND HENRY riled up the yellowjackets in the trash can during lunch and raced around karate-chopping and karate-kicking them.

But nothing was fun, or funny, to River.

She got through the afternoon, carrying with her a big, hollow feeling deep in her belly. When she went home, she would check the driver's guide for other clues. How much was pregnancy counseling? she wondered. The price of two dinners in a restaurant?

Of course!

Anton and Megan weren't going to Chinatown for a birthday dinner. They were going to 123 Thyme Street for an evening pregnancy counseling session. You didn't exactly have to be Sherlock Holmes to figure out what was going on in Megan's life.

River's stomach took a fast dip. What if she saw "abrtn." written somewhere in Megan's handwriting in the driver's pamphlet? What a thought!

She decided never to think it again.

She pretended to sleep during the bus ride home so that Margaret wouldn't talk to her.

She walked down the sidewalk with a couple of kids, but she didn't talk to either one.

The Taurus wasn't in the driveway.

She wandered up the path and into the house and dumped her pack onto the kitchen floor. She opened the refrigerator door and peered in, hoping to see some pasta salad, a pickle and a turkey sandwich with mustard and light mayo waiting for her.

"What's wrong with *you*?" she heard her mother say to Megan.

"What's *wrong*?" cried Megan. "I can't believe you painted my hippie dresser!"

"But you asked me to paint the dresser!" said her mother.

"Not that dresser!"

"What dresser, then?" said her mother. "It's the only dresser in your room!"

Megan closed her eyes. "Mom," she said. She opened her eyes and stared at her mother for a moment before speaking. "The dresser in my closet."

"There's a dresser in your closet?" Their mother

looked in the closet. "That's a bookshelf, Megan. Not a dresser."

"Well, I keep my sweaters on it, don't I?" said Megan.

Their mother turned to River. "I spent the whole day painting this dresser with beautiful glossy nontoxic acrylic paint I got on sale."

"Where's Dad?" asked River.

"Oh. Where's Dad? Let me report that the airport in Reno has been closed due to high winds," said their mother. "So your father isn't home, and won't be home in time for our meeting. I'll have to go by myself."

River looked at her mother's clogs; they were speckled with black dots. "You're going to a meeting in *those shoes?*" said River.

Megan sat down on her bed. "I loved that dresser," she said quietly. Now she was beginning to cry. "I've been looking at the flowers on that dresser from my bed since I was, like, five years old!"

River turned from the doorway. "And now they're gone," she heard Megan say, with her voice trembling. "They'll always be gone. I can't ever get them back! You painted out my childhood."

River went into her room and closed the door behind her. She heard her mother's voice and her sister's voice, but she couldn't hear what they were saying anymore. Suddenly she heard Megan shout, "All I ever ask you is to stay out of my room and leave my stuff alone!"

"Well, pardon the hell out of me!" River heard their mother shout back.

The house grew quiet. Then River heard their mother walk into the hall. She heard Megan slam her door, and then she heard a thump. Megan had probably thrown a sneaker at the door. River had seen tread marks on the back of Megan's door before.

No, there was no way their mother knew that Megan was pregnant. Nobody would be upsetting somebody pregnant like that, or swearing like that around a pregnant teen. River came out of her room. Her mother was standing at the mirror, putting on lipstick. "Boy, your sister's a grump," she whispered to River.

"Mom?" said River.

"What."

"Why are you painting things and messing around in all the closets? How come you painted my sister's dresser without asking?"

"She asked me to!"

"She loved those flowers! You don't even know what's going on with your own family."

"Oh, please."

"You don't!" said River. "I've been noticing you lately! You're in a zone, Mom. You sing to yourself. Yesterday I saw you whirling around in the garden. You think nobody sees you acting like that? With your arms in the air. Who were you dancing with?"

"I was dancing with a finch."

"I believe it," said River.

"I should be able to dance a little outside in my own garden without being spied on and criticized."

"With a bird?" said River. "Anyway," she went on, in a nicer way. "Mom?"

"What."

"When are you going to Price Club again?"

"*What* is it that you and Megan want to eat and drink that we don't seem to have? I just spent two hundred and thirty-eight dollars at Food 4 Less! Why would I go to Price Club?"

"Well, when did you *last* go to Price Club?"

"I don't know, exactly. I suppose it's been a couple of months. I need to stay away from these places. We're going broke saving money."

"Okay," said River politely. "I was just asking."

A couple of months, thought River. It had been at least two months since Megan had had a period. No wonder that purple Kotex box had never been opened!

When would this baby be due? River sat down and put both her hands on her knees and sneakily counted forward through the months on her fingers, moving them ever so slightly, the way she'd been doing in math ever since first grade. September, maybe?

"Honey?" said her mother as she quickly ran a comb through her hair.

River looked up.

"What are you thinking?"

"Nothing," said River.

"What did you need at Price Club?"

"Nothing," said River. Pampers, she thought. About four thousand of them.

"I'll be home soon," said her mother.

"Mom? You know those duck decals—the walking baby duckies walking behind the mama duckie? With the umbrellas?"

Her mother frowned at her.

"On the headboard of my bed?"

"Yes . . ."

"Well, I know you weren't planning to paint anything in my room, but just in case. I really like baby things, like baby duckies and baby skunks. So don't paint out anything baby!"

River went back into her room. She turned the radio way, way down. Was Megan crying? She listened more carefully. She heard Megan's door open; she heard the back door open and shut. With a bang! River walked over and peered through the blinds. She could see Megan wandering across the lawn. Megan sat on the lawn swing and looked at her feet.

River turned from the window. She went into the kitchen. She had a heavy feeling in her stomach that didn't go away even after she had drunk a Coke and burped. She called Candace.

"Can I call you back?" said Candace. "Jules is on the other line."

"Sure," said River. "Bye."

What would Candace and Jules think when they found out River's sister was pregnant?

River went back into her room to spy on Megan again. Megan *couldn't* have stayed a virgin, the way she'd said she was going to do, and gotten pregnant, the way the Virgin Mary did.

Gosh.

Megan and Anton.

Those two dopes!

River's mother had gone out on the porch.

"Well, remember," River heard her call to Megan, "you'd better be back from Chinatown on time! You're a grumpbucket! A frightful grumpbucket and you must be overtired!"

River watched her mother clop down the path to the car. What terrible shoes!

She glanced back at the lawn swing.

Megan was gone.

Maybe she'd run away!

River heard the back door swing open and slam shut.

She heard Megan's door close.

Thank God! thought River. She waited a few minutes. Then she softly knocked on Megan's door. "Megan?" she whispered.

Megan turned the handle to unlock the door and then sat back down on the rug, where she was making small flashcards with French words on them.

River opened it and walked in. She sat down. "I'm going to take Spanish," she told Megan.

"Oh yeah?"

"Yup. French is too hard. Spanish is easier—"

"Shhh!" said Megan.

"—as well as 'more likely to open up job opportunities on the West Coast,' " said River, "according to Jules, who knows a lot about jobs."

River took a deep breath.

"How does Jules know about jobs?" said Megan.

River shrugged.

"Well, I'm going to move to Paris," said Megan.

"When?" said River. She took another deep breath.

Megan shrugged. Then she looked at River. "What are you—hyperventilating?"

"Me?" said River. "No. Why?"

Calm down, River told herself. "Megan?" she said.

"What," said Megan.

Just say it, River told herself.

The phone rang. "Can you get out, please?" Megan said. "It's Anton. We've been fighting."

River wandered back into her room.

Megan and Anton were already fighting and they weren't even married yet!

River heard a soft meow. Helene had gotten in somehow. She'd gotten in and had crept into River's black mailbox in the closet and was sitting on top of the clothes.

River really needed to wash a load.

"Come on, Helene. Out you get!" said River. She picked up Helene and gently put her on the rug, but Helene hung on to River's sheer white nightie and dragged it partway out with her claws. River noticed that—yikes! Her nightgown had a spot of blood on it. Right in the middle of the back.

Oh my gosh! She'd started her period last night! And hadn't noticed! Her nightgown had a blood spot just like she'd seen once on the back of Megan's pajamas. And this morning River had been in such a rush she hadn't even noticed.

She unbuttoned her jeans and checked her undies. No blood. Thank heavens! She'd started and ended her period in the middle of the night.

That was quick.

She hitched her jeans back up.

She went over the Furley instructions for getting blood out of nightgowns, while her heart raced and Helene sat on the rug, meowing and twitching her tail.

She would get the blood out with cold water.

But first she'd mark the calendar!

River hurried into the kitchen and rummaged through the drawer for the calendar. She would mark the day she started with a small dot, per Furley's instructions, so she could keep track. She flipped through the months, stopping in February. Wait a minute. Where were the underpants she'd slept in?

Probably in the hamper, soaked with blood!

River went back into her room. She gingerly took the nightgown the rest of the way out of the mailbox hamper. There, underneath it, bloody and wet, four newborn kittens lay breathing and bobbing their heads. "Megan!" cried River. "Help!" But Megan didn't hear her.

River put her hand on her chest. Helene, *right* on the rug, was squeezing out another kitten. Or meowing it out, somehow. It was black, yellow and white—a calico! River could see it moving its tiny paws inside a sort of wet, see-through sac. "Help!" cried River again.

And Megan came running in.

"Kittens!" cried River. She held on to Megan's arm. They watched Helene lick the kitten, and then—sick!—Helene leaned down and began eating something bloody: the afterbirth, which had come out of . . . Good heavens! Did cats have vaginas?

"Put the kitten with the other ones!" whispered River. "I scared Helene out of her nest!"

"Helene will take care of it," said Megan in a serious way. "It's not up to you so stay out of it."

They tiptoed out and closed the door.

"I practically started my period over that cat!" River whispered to Megan.

"What?"

"Nothing!" said River.

She picked up the calendar. She felt a little disappointed that she wouldn't be marking the first day of her first period on the calendar with a dot.

For about one second.

Instead, she would be marking another memorable event: the birth of Helene's kittens.

Fourteen

RIVER FOUND THE date on the calendar. The box was empty, except for something very small written in pencil in tiny letters in the corner of the box:

"P. T. rslts."

River's heart sank. In her excitement over the kittens, she'd almost allowed herself to forget. "P. T. rslts.": pregnancy test results.

It made River feel sick to her stomach to think of it: Megan being pregnant and hiding it from a family that never had secrets.

River felt a wave of nausea. She sat down at the kitchen table.

She dragged her pack toward her and plopped it on the tabletop. She unzipped the center section and pulled out her Human Interaction notebook. She opened it up and flapped through it, scattering loose papers. She found her Options for a Pregnant Teenager worksheet and briefly reviewed the list.

She stopped to think about whether or not she should underline the option about having the baby and raising the baby with the help of the family.

River tucked the folded paper into the front of her shirt, partway inside her bra—against her heart.

"Can I come in?" she said outside Megan's door.

Megan sighed. "I guess."

River sat on the rug. Megan was making more flash cards for French, and River watched. "Don't you have homework?" asked Megan.

"Candace signed up for a baby-sitting class at the rec center," said River.

"Good for Candace," said Megan. "Can you tell me this later? Anton's coming over right after his test, and then we're leaving. I've got to get this done!"

"The class teaches about CPR and all kinds of safety things," said River. "And how to feed and change a baby, and how to not let the baby roll off the edge of the changing table." Megan stared at the list of words in her book. "And to not ever leave the baby in the bath, not even for one second. Just let the phone ring!" said River. "Never mind the phone until the baby is secure. You can get a certificate at the end of the program."

Megan searched through her cards. "Did I do

pommes frites?" She wrote *pommes frites* on a card. "Fried apples," she mumbled. "Ick."

"And Megan? It shows kids about burping a baby and putting something on your shoulder first. . . ."

"Is it fried apples or french fries?" mumbled Megan. She turned to the back of her French book.

River could see that Megan wasn't really listening. She put her hand on Megan's arm. "And you know what else?"

"Why are your hands so cold?" said Megan. "Your hands are like ice!"

River took her hand off Megan's arm and jammed both of her hands between her knees. "It tells the ten things little kids most often choke on—peanuts and hot dogs and raisins and popcorn I think and a few other things."

"You must be catching what I had," said Megan.

God, I hope not! thought River. You can't catch being pregnant from somebody.

Could you?

Get ahold of yourself! River thought. You're going crazy! Crazy! Nobody can get pregnant from borrowing their sister's toothbrush!

"Does your stomach feel okay?" said Megan. She put her hand on River's cheek. "Maybe we should take your temperature."

"I feel fine," River said. "There's nothing wrong with my stomach. And Megan?" Tears sprang into River's eyes. "I want you to know that I would never let you down."

"Well, I wouldn't let you down either, Riv," said Megan.

The corners of River's mouth kept going down on their own; River struggled to control them. "And I want you to know that I'm perfectly capable of taking care of a baby," said River in a shaky voice. "I like the idea of having a baby."

"Having a *baby*?" said Megan.

"Well, why not?" said River.

"River!" said Megan. "You can't be serious!" They stared at each other. "It's not like having a litter of kittens, I hope you know," said Megan, "where they suddenly just appear in a mailbox full of dirty clothes."

"I know, but—"

"You have to leave school, River! You wouldn't be able to go anyplace without bringing the baby along. You can't even take a baby to the movies! They cry through the whole show!"

"Jules and Candace would help. I'm sure of it!"

"You're twelve years old!" cried Megan. "Twelve. Do you think you could be responsible for a baby?"

"Yes!"

"Well, what I think is that Mrs. Furball or whatever her name is has made you crazy to think somebody can have a baby when they're not even grown themselves."

"I'm only saying . . . Please, Megan! Read through the choices."

River took the folded paper out of her shirt and

opened it up on the rug. "See? Four choices. Mrs. Furley said."

Megan stared at the list of Options for a Pregnant Teenager.

"There isn't anything to be ashamed of, Megan," said River. "We're a family!"

Megan searched River's face.

Then River said, "If you wanted to have a baby I'd stand by you. I'd stand by you no matter what." Her bottom lip moved again and made dimples in her chin. She kept her mouth as tight as she could, and in a second or two she had gained control. Almost.

"We're sisters, Megan!" said River. "We're in it for the long haul!" Tears dribbled down her cheeks.

"River?" said Megan. She gently put her hand on the side of River's face. "You're really starting to scare me. You need to tell me what's going on."

Okay, thought River. She gathered herself. "You think I don't know about morning sickness?" she began. "I know about morning sickness and pregnancy counseling and tough decisions."

"No you don't!" said Megan. "No one your age can know what it means to be pregnant!"

River suddenly grew angry. "Don't pretend you're going to Chinatown with Anton!" she cried. "At least, don't pretend stuff like that with me. Chinatown. For a birthday dinner. What a joke! You may not tell me what's going on anymore, because you spend all your time with your boyfriend. But I know where you and Anton are really going this afternoon; I saw the calendar. And I saw what you wrote in the driver's guide."

"What I wrote in *what* driver's guide?" said Megan.

"The teen handbook!"

Megan got up. She stormed out of the room.

River ran after her.

And half an hour later, they were sitting quietly in the kitchen waiting for their mother to walk in.

"Great news!" cried River the minute she walked through the door. "Helene had kittens!"

"Where is she?" asked their mother.

"In my mailbox," said River.

"River thought I was pregnant," said Megan. "She saw 'P. T. rslts.' written in your calendar. Can you believe it? She thought I was sick to my stomach because I was pregnant."

"Well, sor-ry!" said River.

"She noticed that I never opened the box of Kotex. Can you imagine? It's like the CIA around here. Like I'm being secretly investigated. She didn't think of tampons."

"You are *not* supposed to sleep with a tampon," said River. "You are supposed to use a pad at night—you can ask Mrs. Furley."

"Calm down," said River's mother. "Please!" She frowned. "You're not supposed to sleep with a tampon? I didn't know that!"

"Well, try reading the tampon package!" said River.

"Brother!" said Megan. "Suddenly the world's expert. Aunt River."

"Stop making fun of me," said River. "I'm sick of you making fun of me!"

"You won't believe this!" said Megan to her mother. "When I wrote down the directions for the Department of Motor Vehicles, '*left* past family planning clinic, something or another Thyme Street,' Harriet the Spy here thought I was going for pregnancy counseling with Anton!"

"I'm leaving," said River. She stood up.

"Wait!" said Megan. "Don't go."

Megan looked into their mother's eyes. "Mom? What *does* 'P. T. rslts.' stand for, anyway?"

River's mother sat down.

She looked at Megan, then at River.

She sat with her elbow on the table and her chin in her hand.

She looked at Megan again, and then at River again.

"Mom!" said Megan. "You are not!"

Her mother nodded. "Yes, I am. Daddy and I decided not to mention it until we got results from some tests I had to have done. I've just been to the doctor and we've gone over the results. The baby is fine." She shut her eyes. "Thank God." She opened her eyes.

"Dad and I planned to go to the doctor together this afternoon. He's probably still sitting at the airport, waiting for the storm to blow over. We expected to have this conversation as a family."

River said nothing; she just kept looking at her mother. "*You* are having a baby?" she said after a long pause.

Her mother nodded. "A boy."

"When?"

"In July."

"Let me see your belly," said River.

Her mother lifted her shirt. "It doesn't show yet, but I'll tell you something: Every once in a while, I feel a little flutter. A little flutter inside, like a butterfly's wings. . . ."

"This is *so* unbelievable," said Megan.

"I hope you know that every time somebody looks at you they're going to be thinking about what you and Dad were doing," said River.

"They'll get over it," said her mother.

"I can't believe my mother could get pregnant accidentally at age forty-three!" said Megan.

"Neither can I," said her mother. "But I *thought* I'd gone through menopause."

"I think I need to lie down," said Megan.

"That's *so* great, Mom!" said River. "Good job." She kissed her mother and squeezed her face against her mother's face. "Pick up your shirt again!"

Her mother lifted her shirt.

River rested her ear against her mother's belly. "I can't hear anything," she whispered.

"Well, he's in there. I have a picture to prove it." Her mother took an envelope out of her purse. Inside was a small, square piece of paper with a black-and-white image on it. "See?" she whispered. "He's sucking his thumb!"

The girls frowned at the picture.

"Yup," said their mother. "There's going to be another kid in the coatrack. There's going to be another kid brushing the cat's teeth with your father's toothbrush."

Ick, thought River.

Cat-tooth tartar and scum from those awful little yellow pointy teeth of Helene's . . . on your toothbrush!

Suddenly River's stomach felt weird, but other than that, she'd never felt better. Or happier! She gazed at the picture. Now, where was the thumb? Oops! Now her stomach felt really queasy and icky.

Obviously she'd caught Megan's flu. She raced out and gagged over the porch rail.

Next time she'd use her own toothbrush.

She took a few deep breaths of air and looked up. What an amazing afternoon! A few pink clouds drifted across the blue. Under this same sky, her dad was waiting. He'd call soon and hear the news. A baby brother! Her dad would be so happy to have another boy around! Two boys, surrounded by girls.

Unless there were boy kittens. How could she tell a boy cat from a girl cat?

River didn't know.

Maybe she'd make her handwriting look like Margaret's and write down this question and sneak it into Mrs. Furley's question box.

River breathed an enormous sigh.

She was relieved and happy and reassured.

She'd go into the bathroom, rip open the gigantic box of Kotex pads and take one for a spin!

And she'd snag one for Margaret, while she was at it. Why not take a pad for a spin, and pretend?

River was still a little kid who liked to pretend.

And even after she started her period for real, she would still be a little kid. She'd still be a little kid, with two best friends and a big sister who wasn't pregnant.

And a little brother.

Who could flutter like a butterfly.

And a dad who poked holes in the desert.

And a mom who danced with a finch.

She glanced down the street. A big truck was rumbling toward her. Behind it was a brand-new jet-black convertible Jeep with a roll bar and fat, muddy tires.

"Dad's home!" cried River.

Her father drove over the curb and up onto the lawn. His hair was blown back over his bald spot; his collar was up. He looked a little like Robert Redford, only dirtier.

He jumped out in muddy boots and wrinkled chino pants—and a shirt that looked as if he'd slept in it.

He reached back in and took out a pink box tied with string, with a circle of grease on the top. He held it up. "Lemon meringue pie!" he called.

"Sick!" cried River. She leaned over the rail and gagged again. She imagined the awful, fluffy

130

peaked egg goop that was undoubtedly wiggling on the top of the pie. "Put it back in the car!" she yelled.

River's mom came outside and walked down the steps. She said something quietly to River's dad.

Then River's parents stood on the path and hugged for a very long time. Megan wandered out. She and River stood on the porch, watching.

They saw their mom and dad kiss.

Gross!

Then they watched their mom show their dad the little picture of the baby.

Their dad found his glasses in his shirt pocket and unfolded them and put them on. And, a moment later, River saw something she'd never seen before: Two tears made two lines through the dust on her dad's face from the corners of his eyes down to where the stubble of his beard began.

What a good dad he was—to roar home all the way from Reno to try to make it back in time for the meeting with the doctor.

With that horrible pie!

And a very handsome crybaby dad he was—and very dapper in his geologist duds and stolen company Jeep!

Or borrowed, or whatever it was.

River moved closer to Megan. "After Mom has this baby," River said quietly, "*if* you get your license and your Honda with tinted windows, let's drive those two to the family planning clinic for some birth control."

"For sure," said Megan.

They linked arms.

"And I also think we should enroll them in Mrs. Furball's sex class," said Megan.

River looked up at Megan.

Megan was smiling!

"Can I borrow your lipstick?" said River.

About the Author

Mavis Jukes won a Newbery Honor Book citation for *Like Jake and Me* and is the author of numerous other books, including *Blackberries in the Dark, Getting Even, Wild Iris Bloom,* and *It's a Girl Thing.* She lives with her husband, an artist, in California. This is her first book for Delacorte Press.